J.P. CHOQUETTE

Hear No Evil

First published by Scared E Cat Books 2021

Copyright © 2021 by J.P. Choquette

All rights reserved. No part of this publication may be reproduced, stored or transmitted in any form or by any means, electronic, mechanical, photocopying, recording, scanning, or otherwise without written permission from the publisher. It is illegal to copy this book, post it to a website, or distribute it by any other means without permission.

This novel is entirely a work of fiction. The names, characters and incidents portrayed in it are the work of the author's imagination. Any resemblance to actual persons, living or dead, events or localities is entirely coincidental.

NOTE: This book was previously published under the name "Restitution".

First edition

ISBN: 978-1-950976-16-4

This book was professionally typeset on Reedsy.
Find out more at reedsy.com

Note to Readers

This book was previously published under the name "Restitution" in 2015.

Chapter One

I walk up the stairs to my office, praying they won't give out. The stairs are sketchy-bordering-on-dangerous. Plus, I'm carrying an extra fifteen pounds since I last made this climb.

The phone in my office rings. Fifteen more stairs and I'll be at the door. I imagine a new client on the other end. A client with money to offset the recent debts I've racked up. A client who expects a fit, strong, security professional to pick up the phone. I push myself to move faster, wishing the extra weight was due to a couple of heavy bags of office supplies. It's not. Avoiding mirrors for the past two months doesn't disguise the fact that none of my pants fit anymore. Sweatpants, while comfy and soft, are not a good measure of one's mass.

Go figure.

Huffing and puffing up the last two steps, I fumble with keys outside my office door. *T.R. Waters Securities* is emblazoned in gold letters across the frosted glass. The T.R. stands for Tatum Rose, but only my mother, a Southern belle, calls me that. To everyone else, I'm Tayt. Finally getting the door open, I launch myself across the room and grab the phone on the last ring.

"T.R. Waters Securities, this is Tayt."

There's a click and then a low buzz of static before a voice comes on the line.

"Oh, er, hello there," a male voice says. "My name is Phil and I'm happy to be calling you from the bright island of Bermuda today." Pause. A long, low toot of a big ship fills the line. Mechanical-sounding gulls fill in the space before the man's voice starts again.

"Ms. Waters, I'm calling today on behalf of Tropical Cruise Lines, excited to tell you about—"

"I'm sorry," I say, phone halfway to the cradle. "I'm not interested. Thanks, anyway."

Click.

The truth is I *am* interested. Who wouldn't want to scurry off to a beach and sport a lobster-like sunburn this time of the year? Snow falls outside the big windows across the room as I put away my winter coat and remove my dripping boots. In their place, I slip on my favorite pair of combat boots, featuring the London Jack over each toe. My footwear, at least. is not compromised by my new, larger size.

As I tie the boots, I think about a cruise. Jetting off into the sunset—the warm, coconut-scented sunset—sounds pretty good. Self-employed startups don't take a lot of vacation days, though. My company—and by company, I mean me—manages everything from working as extra security at a local concert to tracking down missing persons to spying on one's significant other for means of proving infidelity. Plus, a handful of jobs that I don't advertise.

The phone rings again as soon as I fire up my laptop. I sigh, look at the caller ID, and see "out of area." I could ignore it. But I don't.

"T.R. Waters Securities, this is Tayt."

"Please don't hang up," Phil's voice again, but this time soft and desperate-sounding. The line is clear, crisp. "I'm calling you from my cell. I'm in the storage closet at work. I need your help."

"Okaaay," I say, drawing the word out. "What can I do for you?"

"It's my…" His voice fades to a whisper. Either that, or he's moved his mouth too far from the phone to hear.

"What? Sorry, I lost you there," I say. I hear a door open and close on the other end.

Phil clears his throat.

"I'll have to call you back, Mom." His voice is so loud in my ear that I yank the phone away a few inches. He continues, "Yes, I know. Love you too!"

There's a click and I sit there a minute before realizing he's hung up on me.

Weird.

There is too much on my plate today to spend time worrying about it. I've been able to keep up (mostly) with the T.R. Waters Securities website while in recovery. Nothing like a gunshot wound to the shoulder to help one focus on priorities. Having a lot of time on my hands—seven weeks, two days, and something like seventeen hours—was good for one thing and one thing only: deciding what needs to stay and what needs to go, work-wise.

For the past several years I've owned and operated a cleaning business, Repo Renew, which is exactly what it sounds like; I clean foreclosed homes and prepare them for a realtor to stage. But, while the money was decent, I got little enjoyment from it. A change was needed. So I'd opened a securities business. The economy in the toilet, zilch experience—what could go wrong with this new venture?

Despite a rocky start, the business is growing. In fact, I'm ready to commit to T.R. Waters Securities and let Repo Renew go—at least the day-to-day management piece of it, which has been covered very well by Cindy Sheldon. She's a ball of energy and enjoys the work. I enjoy the fact that she's competent and self-motivated and not one of those people who has to call a zillion times a day with dumb questions like, "Do I use paper towels or rags on the glass?"

I lean back in my chair and stretch my arms overhead. Well, I only get halfway before my shoulder screeches. I let my arms fall and rub the area where the bullet had penetrated. Never in a million years had I expected to find myself trapped in a cabin in the middle of nowhere, being shot at. I frown, feeling the scar even through the fabric of my shirt. Will it ever heal fully?

Not if you don't slow down, an annoying little voice pipes up in my head.

Ignoring it, I bring up my email account and scroll through, tossing the ads for penis-enlarging supplements and expensive watches and checking for legit requests. Three emails sent directly through my site's "Contact Us" form stick out. I open the first.

"Please help me get my boyfriend back. I don't know where he is. I'm desperate for help and the police won't listen to me. I can pay you big money!! Here is my contact information..." I jot down the woman, Sandra Garrison's, phone number and email address while simultaneously rubbing my neck.

Relationship cases are the worst. So much angst to so few satisfying results in most cases. If I'm successful, the missing boyfriend/girlfriend/fiancé/husband or wife will be found.

But most often it's *who* he or she's found *with* that causes the heartbreak. Still, Visa and MasterCard will appreciate the job.

I frown and bite my lip. That name is familiar. Garrison. Garrison… The tickle of remembrance floats away.

Puffing my cheeks out with a sigh, I open the second request. This one is from a man whose first name is Phil. The same guy who just called on the phone? He left no last name, just the initial "H," and his message is cryptic at best: "Please contact at your earliest convenience."

I jot down his number. There's no email address.

The final request is from Julia Lawson who states only that she needs security help for a weekend event. There's no date listed as to when the event is scheduled.

Please, not this weekend.

I rub my shoulder again.

Opening my bag, I find my trusty day planner and flip through the weeks of missed work. Appointments had to be canceled—most farmed out to other freelancers or bigtime security companies in Burlington. I hated to lose the jobs and the money, but what can you do when you're flat on your back?

I turn to today's date on the calendar and make a pact with myself: fill next week's blocks with new business and I can treat myself to a little shopping spree. Glancing at my stretchy knit pants, I frown. Better make the goal to fill the next two weeks' time slots with new gigs. Mama needs a new wardrobe at this point.

I open and pay bills then sort paperwork for a little while. The predictability is soothing. Taking a break, I water the plants, glad I chose hardy succulents. My green thumb is only in effect at my house, not the office. After that, I run a duster around the equipment and coffee cart, sweep the floor (poorly, because my chest is starting to ache), then settle at my green metal desk with a cup of coffee and the phone. Time to drum up some new business.

I call the phone number for Phil first, but the line just rings and rings. Who doesn't have voicemail in this day and age? I make a note to try again later and punch in the number for Julia Lawson. A woman's voice answers on the third ring. She sounds middle-aged, rotund, and smiley.

"Ms. Lawson, this is Tayt Waters from T.R. Waters Securities. You contacted us via our website and I'm returning your call."

A little laugh.

"Oh, my, yes. That was me, wasn't it?"

I roll my eyes, glad (yet again) that phones don't come with built-in video projectors.

"Seems like it, ma'am."

"Well, it just so happens that my son is in a band? And he's going to be playing music at a house party in Colchester? We'd hoped to hire your firm for security purposes?"

Every sentence ends on the upswing, as though she's asking question after question. I grit my teeth silently and force a smile onto my face.

"Yes, that's something we should be able to help with. And what is the date of the event?"

Not this weekend. Not this weekend. I touch the aching spot with three fingers and rub.

"This week. Friday night, starting around eight o'clock? Can your boss, Mr. Waters, do that?"

I clear my throat.

"I am the boss, ma'am; Tayt Waters." Silence on the other end. "And yes, I'd be happy to help at this event."

Long pause.

Then, "But you're a woman." Finally, a sentence that actually sounds like a sentence, ignorant though it is.

"Don't worry. I know my stuff. I have my black belt and have been practicing martial arts since I was a kid. I have references as well. If you'd like to speak with them…"

She interrupts, a laugh mixing in with her words.

"I saw many good testimonials on your website? It sounds like you know what you're doing?"

Ack! How can I get off the phone before throwing it through the window? *Deep breath.* I don't have to like my clients, I just have to do a good job and not blurt out anything rude before they pay me.

I grimace, hoping it comes across like a smile in my voice.

"Thanks. Let me just open up my program here and I'll get all the pertinent information from you."

I jot down notes while Mrs. Lawson goes on and on about her talented son, a singer-drummer-songwriter who is just so, well, *talented* she can hardly stand it. I murmur a lot of "uh-huhs" and "mmms" into the phone and finally, blessedly, have the information I need. I promise to email her the contract and Julia agrees to sign it and return it with the deposit.

"Thank you so much? It's been a pleasure?"

I sing-song a thank you to her and hang up before she can ask me another statement.

No sooner do I replace the receiver than the phone rings again. Out of area number. Maybe Phil again? I answer with my standard greeting while fumbling to grab a fresh contract form out of the file cabinet for Mrs. Lawson.

There's no answer at first to my *hello-this-is-Tayt* spiel. I'm about to say hello again when a distorted mechanical voice fills the silence.

"I'm watching you."

I glance up, look around my office as though the person is standing there looking at me. There is heavy breathing on the other end of the phone. My heartbeat thumps hard in my chest, banging against my ribs like a bird trying to escape its cage.

I rack my brain for something clever to say but only manage to squeak out an, "Oh, really?"

There is a mechanical, grating sound on the other end. Laughter?

"I'm watching you. You'll pay for hurting me."

Chapter Two

I slam the receiver down, as though that's going to show the caller who's boss; never mind that he or she has already hung up. Letting out a breath, I push my chair away from the desk and stand.

"I'm watching you" and "you'll pay" are classic teen-slasher movie threats. Likely just a dumb kid playing a prank. The butterflies in my belly don't agree. Just for fun, I try a number combination on the phone to try and track the call. It doesn't work.

Immediately, my mind goes to my Sunflower Specials, a little side business where I help people, mostly women, which the criminal justice system has failed. But the caller dialed my work line, not the separate burner phone I keep specifically for the Specials. I think about the language of the caller. Educated? Hard to tell. Not very old. Or maybe that, too, was changed with the mechanical sound effects?

Shake it off. I sigh and sit back down. Creating a file for Mrs. Lawson is my first task. Dorky but true, I like the administrative part of running my own business. Once the shiny ink has dried on the new label and the contract is filled in and emailed, I go on to my next phone call. Sandra

Garrison, the woman with the missing boyfriend. *Ugh.* My last relationship-gone-wrong case was a real tear-jerker if you believe in true love and all that crap.

Sandra answers on the fifth ring just as I'm about to hang up. Her greeting is bubbly and warm as she answers, "Garrison's gym." I hadn't realized it was *that* Garrison. No wonder the name sounded familiar. I stumble over my introduction, but she doesn't seem to notice. Her voice when responding is two octaves lower, though.

"I can't talk right now, it's super busy this morning. Can I meet you somewhere later today?"

"Sure." I pull my appointment book back out. The boxes are depressingly empty. "What time works for you?"

"Um, I'll be done here around…" her voice fades for a moment, then, "Oh, hey, Wanda! Looking good!" Her voice is at a nearly screaming level. "Sorry about that. New client. They need lots of encouragement." She laughs. "Two o'clock work?"

"Sure."

"We can meet at Juice Bar; it's the smoothie place on Main Street."

"Perfect," I say, grimacing and making a mental note to eat lunch before then. I've seen the strange pond-water-colored beverages coming out of that place.

"See you then!" she practically yells into the phone, heavy bass thumping in the background.

***

I spend another hour at the office and try Phil one more time, but, again, the phone just rings and rings. I get out a new contract sheet for Sandra, just in case our late afternoon meeting goes well and she wants to hire me on the spot. Then I lock up and make my way down the creaking stairs to the street. It's cold and a light snow is still falling, the flakes so small they look like glitter. The scents of snow and wood smoke and undertones of exhaust fill the air.

I glance at the old, white, Victorian house across the street and think of my friend Alinah. Can it be only a couple of months since I've seen her? It seems like a lifetime ago. I wonder how she's doing in Malaysia. The last time we spoke she was doing well. I'm happy for her.

The weather must be better there, I think as a gust of cold air winds around my coat collar and pokes at my neck. I hunch my shoulders and walk quickly to the rear parking lot. There sits my sad-looking Toyota, rusted and as rundown as the parking lot itself, which is filled with potholes and buckling pavement. I pat the hood of the trusty car and open the door, which squawks in protest. Waiting for the engine to reheat itself after a couple of hours in the cold, I plan out the rest of my day.

First, a stop at the gym—not Garrison's; I go to a martial arts and boxing place in a seedier part of town. It's been weeks now and I haven't done so much as a leg lift. How am I ever going to get back to my "fighting weight" and regain any strength if I don't start moving?

But then my stomach whines and grumbles. I'm starving. I can't work out on an empty stomach, right? Okay then, new plan: lunch first. An early one, since it's only eleven o'clock. Then a couple of annoying errands and a quick workout before I meet with Sandra.

Chapter Three

Main Street in St. Albans is bustling when I pull into a parking spot at one-thirty for my afternoon appointment. Lunch was eaten, my errands were run, and now I'm half an hour early. That's okay, though, I brought along a work-related task to tackle. I haul my canvas messenger bag into the restaurant with me.

Juice Bar is a busy place. Baristas hand freshly-made, raw meals and tall glasses of smoothies over a glass case to a mix of business professionals and twenty-somethings. Snagging one of the last free tables, I decide to wait to place my order until after Sandra arrives. Maybe she can help me navigate the menu. It's my first time here, my culinary tastes veering more toward burgers and fries than raw crepes and odd-sounding combinations of vegetables and fruits mushed together.

After pulling off my coat, I reach into the side pocket of my bag and take out a flip phone. This phone number is not listed on my business cards or website; it's reserved for Sunflower Specials. I turn the phone over in my hands a few times while staring out the window. The snowflakes have gotten fatter, leaving a layer of white fluff over newspaper boxes and car roofs. Finally, I open the flip phone and put my finger on the button which will turn it on.

But I don't press. Biting my lip, I leave my finger there. I should check messages, at least.

But do I need more stress at this point?

I don't have to call anyone back.

Of course, then I'll have to deal with the guilt. Whereas, if I don't turn the phone on at all...

But I should find out who has called, who needs me.

Shouldn't I?

Before I can push the button, a woman's voice sounds near my elbow.

"Excuse me. Are you Tayt?"

Her voice is loud and I jump, my heart racing. I squirrel the phone away into my bag while simultaneously turning to her.

The woman in front of me is model-beautiful, nearly six feet tall with long, smooth blonde hair that's pulled back from her face.

"I am, yes. You must be Sandra." I stand and put out my hand. Her grip is tight and her handshake is strong. Wearing a puffy, white ski jacket and black exercise tights, she looks ready to slalom to the register to place her order. She smiles and her teeth are very white against her tanned skin.

"It looks like you're in the middle of something. I'm early," she laughs. "Did you need to finish what you're doing before we meet?"

I shake my head. "No, I'm all set."

"Did you place your order yet?"

"Oh, ah, no. Not yet. I'll go up with you."

Extracting my wallet from my bag, I practically jog behind Sandra to keep up. We place our orders at the shiny counter; hers for a raw, Hawaiian, flatbread "pizza" and mine for a

Mango Tango smoothie.

"That's all?" she asks, eyebrows raised. "Oh, are you doing a cleanse?"

I think of the meaty sandwich nearly as big as my head that I'd inhaled for lunch.

"Um, no, I just had lunch."

Sandra gets distracted by the counterperson asking if she wants extra pineapple on her raw pizza and I turn to study the place. It's modern and minimalist-looking, all shiny chrome bars with tall, glossy, orange stools. The lighting is bright but flattering, with no fluorescent bulbs in sight. There are gigantic framed posters on the walls of laughing, healthy-looking people enjoying nature. Each one is thin and athletic-looking. I suck in my stomach, wishing now that I'd made it to the gym after all. *Tonight. I'll definitely go tonight.*

"All set," Sandra says, balancing a turquoise tray on the flat of her palm.

"Oh, I'm sorry. How much do I owe you?"

She waves her other hand, making a *pshaw* sound, and weaves between tables until we are back where we started. "Don't worry about it. If you decide to take the job, this can be your first payment." She places the tray in the center of the table and smiles at me. "Totally kidding."

I smile back.

We take our seats, me pressing myself carefully into the chair and trying to choose a position for my legs that is most flattering. The tiny tabletop doesn't provide much coverage. Sandra draws her legs to the side, striking a pose that is both graceful and effortless.

"So, do you live around here?" she asks, cutting slices of the strangest-looking pizza I've ever seen.

I nod my head.

"Not far."

She nods, taking a bite of the concoction on her plate. I unwrap my paper straw and plunge it into the thick, orangey liquid in front of me. I expect a chalky, fibrous texture. Instead, the drink is as smooth as silk. Very tasty. I take another sip.

"This is pretty good."

"First time here?" she asks, taking a bite of the pizza.

"Is it that obvious?"

She smiles and shakes her head. "Just a guess. My cousin owns the place, so I'm in here all the time. The food is really good; you've got to try this pizza sometime." She pauses, wiping the corner of her mouth with a napkin that is covered in tiny daisies. "I'm happy to share. Would you like a bite of this one?"

"Oh, uh, no, thanks. I'm good. It does look"—I search for a positive adjective—"flavorful, though."

We sit in silence for a couple of minutes, chewing and sipping respectively. Then I break it with a question. "So, you said when you contacted me that your boyfriend is missing. Is that right?"

Sandra finishes chewing her bite, her eyes softening. She wipes her mouth again and nods.

"Yeah. Mark has been gone since Saturday and the police don't seem very concerned about finding him."

"Did you file a missing person's report? Sorry if that sounds like a dumb question, but I want to make sure we've covered the bases."

She nods. "I did. But the cops all seemed disinterested. They gave me the whole 'an adult has the right to leave town without notice' spiel. But that's not like Mark. He always tells me where he's going and when he'll be back."

I pull a notebook and pen from my bag and start taking notes. "When did you see him last?"

"Saturday morning at the gym. I had the early shift that day and he came in around ten for a workout. It got busy before he left so we didn't have much of a chance to talk. I called him later that afternoon to see if he wanted to get together, but he didn't answer. I left a message and then tried again on Sunday. Three times, actually, on Sunday. Still no response."

I frowned. "And he didn't mention anything about going out of town? No work commitment that might have suddenly come up?"

Sandra shakes her head. "He works as a waiter at a local restaurant."

"Oh. Which restaurant is that?"

"Chantal's."

I make a note on my pad. "Have you spoken with his boss?"

Her face looks surprised. "No, I didn't think of that."

"I'll start there. Did you bring a photo along also?"

She digs in the puffy coat's pocket and extracts a small metal case. Clicking it open, she pulls out two photos and slides them over to me. The first shows a handsome man, probably in his mid-thirties, grinning for the camera. It's a shoulder-up shot, but I can tell he's muscular and fit. His hair is brown, his eyes dark. The second picture is of Sandra and Mark together, both shiny with oil, both unnaturally tan, both wearing tiny bikinis and posing, muscles popping.

"That last one was at the bodybuilding show in Burlington last spring. Mark placed first in his class and I came in second in the figure competition."

I go from feeling fat to bloated-whale status. I nod. "Can I keep this one?" I point to the solo shot of Mark.

"Sure. At some point, I'd like it back, though."

"Of course." I tuck the photo into the front cover of the notebook.

"I'll need his contact information: address and phone number, family in the area, plus any other information you can think of. Who he hangs out with, where he likes to spend his free time, that sort of thing."

Sandra finishes chewing another bite and nods. "Anything that will help, just let me know. And whatever you normally charge, you can double it if you find him. I just want to know where he is, that he's safe."

***

I leave shortly after Sandra finishes her lunch. I'm exhausted and it's easy to talk myself out of going to the gym. Instead, I spend the rest of the afternoon reading and puttering around the house. Home has always been my favorite place to be, but after nearly three months straight, it's quickly become the place to begin wall climbing.

After tossing a load of wet stuff in the dryer, I lift a half-full basket of dry laundry onto my hip. My doctor told me that I shouldn't be lifting anything more than a couple of pounds until the healing is complete. But that would involve, what, carrying out pieces of clothes one by one?

I grimace against the pulling feeling in my chest and shoulder and bang through the laundry room door, knocking my bag to the floor in the process. The burner phone falls out, the one that I never checked for voicemail messages.

Chicken, a little voice inside says.

Stepping over it, I set the laundry basket on the counter in the kitchen and retrieve the small phone from the floor. Not that I need to prove that voice wrong, but I dial "1" to listen to new messages.

"You have three new messages," a mechanical-sounding woman tells me. I press the same number again to listen.

Silence. Then some soft country music, then the message ends. I push delete and move on to the next. The second message begins with a kid whining in the background. Then a woman's voice stumbles over a greeting.

"Yes, I don't know who you are but I need your help. Please, my baby girl…" her voice breaks off and I can hear her crying for a moment before it returns. "My daughter, Leanne. I need your help. Please call me." She leaves a number and hangs up, the whining kid in the background gaining volume.

Is she talking about that kid? Shivering as I picture that nanny show on TV, I press the save button, then listen to the last message. This one is filled with static, but then it clears and I hear the same woman's voice.

"Please, call me. My name is Reba—Reba Riddell. My husband doesn't know I'm calling, but my daughter, Leanne, she needs help. Please call." Again, she leaves her phone number.

The mechanical, recorded voice tells me that the call came in two weeks ago and guilt blooms in my chest like algae.

Crap.

Chapter Four

T he next morning is bright and blue, the sky overhead nearly void of clouds. The sun feels good after being MIA for so long, but the air is still frigid. I unlock my office door and turn up the heat dial of the thermostat, leaving my coat and scarf on. Hunching at my desk, I fire up the laptop and open a new file for Sandra Garrison. After that, I start a pot of coffee brewing. I'm just thinking of trying Phil again when the office phone rings.

I go through my regular greeting and—surprise, surprise—Phil happens to be on the other end.

"I tried to call you several times," I say. "I couldn't leave a message—"

"No voicemail. Look, I don't have a lot of time. I'm at work again and my boss is a real jerk. I need to meet with you. There's a situation that I'm dealing with that requires your skills." He clears his throat. "I looked around your website and saw that you offer security details for events, right?"

"Well, yeah, I do, but—"

"I have something in two weeks and I need your help. It's a..." His voice fades out for a moment and I think the call's been disconnected. "It's a private function."

Pause.

I clear my throat. "Phil, do we know each other? Your voice sounds familiar."

There's another moment of silence and then he says, so quietly I can barely hear him, "We graduated in the same class. Phil Hunley."

I nearly clap my hand over my mouth which immediately wants to blurt, "Phil the Pill," which would not only be unprofessional but also inappropriate. In high school, Phil used to wear all black and dark makeup before goth was a thing. He kept stolen prescription medicine on him at all times, sewed into the hems of his clothes. And once, I saw him extract a teeny tiny silver case from his ear with—you guessed it—a couple of teeny tiny pills inside.

"Oh, wow," I manage. "It's been a long time."

Awkward pause.

"Um, well, you said you need security at this event?"

Phil sighs. "I have to go. My boss is out in the hall." His voice is a near whisper and I picture him in a broom closet filled with mop, pail, and cleaning supplies.

"I'll help," I tell him quickly. Honestly, I always felt a little bad for Phil. He didn't have any friends in school. Plus, I've always had a soft spot for loners. Or losers. Maybe both. Probably because I see myself in both camps.

"Great." His voice is relieved. "I'll get in touch soon with more information. Don't bother trying to call unless you keep weird hours. Between work and my side business, I can rarely answer my phone. Gotta go."

He hangs up before I can get out a goodbye.

I sit back in my chair for a few minutes reminiscing on the painful years known as high school. Is there anyone who looks back on that time with honest longing?

Pfft, not me.

I pour my first cup of the day and burn my tongue in my haste to get some caffeine flowing in my veins.

Next, I do the regular morning routine. It feels really good to be "back in the saddle," so to speak. Voicemail messages are nonexistent, but I have jobs in the works already, so this isn't necessarily a bad thing. I check the website and see that traffic is slow. Not surprising, since my marketing efforts have been nil these last several weeks. Making a mental note to work on that, I respond to a couple of emails, then make a bank transfer so that I can pay the utility bills without going into arrears.

Finally, I settle into my first real work of the day, mapping out a plan to find Sandra's beloved, Mark. I make a note to call my ex-turned-friend and state trooper, C.J., and see what the police have been doing as far as the search goes. Odd that I haven't seen anything in the paper. I make another mental note to pick up a copy of today's paper.

While the P.I.s of old might have started with some serious gumshoe tracking, in today's world, social networking is where it's at. I check LinkedIn and Twitter, but Mark has accounts with neither. Facebook, however, is a score. Mark isn't a chatty fellow online, but he is part of a few weightlifting groups and I see that the most recent comment from him was on Saturday. I check geotags and make a note of the longitude and latitude for future reference. No comments on his page other than a few posts on his timeline from Sandra.

"Hey, sweetie, how are you? Call me when you can, 'kay?"

"Mark, where *are* you? Please call me ASAP."

"Mark. Seriously? Call me."

The messages were posted daily between Sunday and yesterday, one per day. I look for his phone number just to see if there's anything listed that Sandra didn't give me, but don't see anything. Most people create privacy settings to hide that information anyway, but it's always worth a shot. Techno-dummies do exist and make my work much easier.

I decide a field trip is in order. After turning off the coffeepot and washing my mug, I go through the whole winter clothes thing in reverse. My combat boots are so worn in and warm that they feel like slippers and I hate to take them off. I do, though, exchanging them for my wool-lined winter boots, pulling the laces tight.

I look longingly toward the rear parking lot after locking up and descending the staircase but turn the other direction and begin my trek up the street, toward the center of St. Albans. If I can't get my ever-expanding bum to the gym, I can at least burn off a few calories by walking.

The air is crisp and cold. My breath makes tiny white clouds as I walk past a shopping plaza, a pharmaceutical company, and cross train tracks where Amtrak deposits and picks up passengers. There aren't many other pedestrians out. In the warmer months, the streets tend to be filled with young moms pushing baby strollers and punks wearing hoodies and yammering into cell phones. I pass Snuffy's on the corner, one of my favorite greasy spoons. The smell of hot fat and something sweet fills my nose and makes my mouth water. Maybe just a little treat…?

I give myself a mental shake and take in Main Street ahead of me. Taylor Park is across the street, covered in snow and showcasing barren trees along with a dull green fountain and a war memorial. At night, the trees are lit with strands of tiny white lights, and around Christmas, a wooden sleigh and reindeer make the park home. Now, though, in mid-January, the park is spartan.

I pass a bank, a series of small shops carrying everything from specialty foods to artwork, a hair salon, and a couple of antique stores. A bookstore on the end of one block is next door to *Chantal's,* a French-inspired restaurant. It's also where Mark Chester works. I try the door and am surprised to find it open; I'd anticipated taking care of a few errands on foot just to kill time until it opened.

The interior is dark, all white-clothed tables and stark artwork on the exposed stone walls. A long, black bar lines the left side of the room, and the smell of food hangs in the air. A lone man stands behind the bar, polishing glasses.

"May I help you?" he asks, pausing mid-wipe.

I head in that direction. "Yes, I hope so. I'm looking for an employee of yours, Mark Chester."

His eyebrows raise and he goes back to wiping, maintaining eye contact. "And you are?"

"Tayt Waters, of T.R. Waters Securities."

He breathes out loudly. "I see."

"Is there a problem?"

"I suppose there must be if you are here, correct?"

His voice has a slight hint of a French accent. He's attractive in a snooty sort of way; longish nose and receding hairline, but his eyes are chocolate-colored and lined with so many dark lashes it looks like he's wearing eye makeup.

"I'm Jean-Pierre, the owner. I haven't seen him since Saturday," he says. "He did not show up for his shift on Sunday afternoon. No call, either, if you were going to ask."

I was, but don't tell him that. Instead, I nod and take my notepad and pen out.

"Is that unusual? Is he a good worker?"

Jean-Pierre shrugs, places the glass he was polishing under the counter, and smooths a hand over his sparse hair.

"He is a good server. He has been here for…let's see…" He studies the ceiling. "Ten months? No, nine months now. No trouble." He glances at me then notices something on the bar and wipes his white towel over it. He rubs and buffs for a few seconds in silence. "Not the best in the world"—(*his* the *sounds like a* zee)—"but I have had worse. None that lasted, of course. This is a top-notch establishment. I do not suffer fools for employees."

I nod, grateful he's not my boss. I'm suddenly very conscious of my less-than-fashionable ensemble. I can practically feel his inner French fashion police glaring at me. If only I fit into something other than these stupid stretchy pants.

"Any idea where he would have gone?" I push thoughts of my appearance to the back of my mind. "Was he friends with any of the other employees?"

He shrugs. "No, no idea where he would have gone. Out west, maybe."

West?

"What makes you think that?"

Jean-Pierre sighs and then looks at me, frowning.

"He talked about it from time to time. Not to me, of course, but I hear everything that is said in this place one way or another." He continues before I can ask another question, "He was interested in cooking. Or, rather, anti-cooking."

"Anti-cooking," I repeat.

"Mmmm, the raw foods diet. You have heard of this?"

I think of Juice Bar and Sandra's entrée. "I have. Some people do that for, like, a living?"

"Apparently." Jean-Pierre sniffs and starts rubbing his white cloth over another glass. "There's a culinary school that specializes in this type of diet in Arizona. Or New Mexico, maybe. Mark wanted to attend. I do not know much more than that, but you might want to speak with Chad, our dishwasher. The two got along well. He is out back now if you would like to speak with him briefly." He looks over the glass at me, emphasizing the word "briefly."

"Thanks, that'd be great," I say and walk toward the door in the rear of the space where his thin finger points.

The kitchen is so bright after the dim interior of the restaurant that I'm nearly blinded. A loud clanking comes from the back of the space covered with stainless steel. The floor is red tile and spotless, along with all of the stainless-steel counters.

I follow the clanking sounds and find a guy in his mid-twenties behind a wall with a pass-through window where dirty dishes are shoved by the busboys. He has long hair in dreadlocks. His arms—roughly the size of small trees—are tattooed up to his t-shirt sleeves and maybe beyond that. He's wearing a baggy but clean t-shirt and equally baggy jeans. He glances my way and blue eyes peer at me from under a bandana rolled to keep the dreads from falling into his eyes. His nose sports a thick metal bull ring.

"Hey," he says. He's propping a huge silver pot in the sink full of bubbles. The pot is big enough for me to sit in.

"Hello," I say. "I'm Tayt Waters. I run a securities firm and was hired to look for Mark Chester. I understand he's missing."

Chad had paused when I gave my greeting, but now he goes back to scrubbing. "Really? Huh."

"Can you tell me when you last saw him?"

"Not sure where he went after Saturday night. We were supposed to get together for an early workout on Sunday, but he never showed."

"This was at Garrison's gym?"

He nods.

"We workout there a few times a week." He pauses again to swipe at a stray dread that's come loose from the bandana. "Who hired you?"

"I'm sorry?"

"Who hired you to find Mark?"

"I'm sorry," I say again. "That information is confidential."

He nods, a small smile forming on his lips. "Then so's any information I could share."

I cross my arms, aware that this body language isn't going to help Chad open up to me. I uncross them and then feel awkward. What body language says "Trust me?"

"Look, I'm not at liberty to discuss my clients, it's a part of my contract. But someone was worried enough to hire me."

Scrub, scrub, scrub.

"Did Mark say anything to you about moving? Maybe out west?"

Chad lifts his head, looks me over. I suck in my stomach unconsciously.

"You work out at Garrison's? You seem familiar."

I shake my head, flattered that he thinks I work out at all. "I use the gym on Weldon Street. Martial arts, mostly."

Chad's eyebrows raise. "You should come to Garrison's sometime. I'm allowed a guest two times a month." Is he asking because he wants to see me again or because he can tell I need a workout? A smile crinkles the corner of his mouth.

"Thanks, but I'm recovering from an injury right now." My

words sound stiff. Worse, my cheeks are getting hot. What is wrong with me?

He nods. "Change your mind, let me know."

"About Mark…"

Chad puts the pot down and wipes his hands on a nearby towel. He stretches his back, dreads dangling halfway down his back. I try not to stare, but they've always fascinated me.

He catches my eye again and now my cheeks are on fire. Has being a hermit for two months made me such a socially awkward person?

"Look, here's what I know about Mark. He's a good guy. I've been here at Chantal's two years and most of the servers here act like dishwashers are lepers or something." He pauses and takes a couple of swigs from a water glass on the stainless-steel shelf over the sink. "Mark was cool. Down to earth, you know? We had our breaks at the same time. It turned out we had a lot in common. I got him interested in weightlifting, he got me turned on to eating healthier. We're buddies, hang out. That's it. We weren't dating or anything, so I don't know all the intricacies of his life."

"Do you know his girlfriend, Sandra?"

Chad, who had just taken a swig of water, nearly spits it out. Instead, he chokes.

I wait for him to finish, then ask again, "Sandra at Garrison's. Do you know her well? Did you and Chad ever, I don't know, double date?"

He shakes his head, pounding one fist on his chest and clearing his throat.

"No," he croaks. "Sandra's—"

"Excuse me."

I hadn't heard Jean-Pierre appear in the kitchen and yet here he is, near my shoulder. I jump and then try to make it appear that he didn't startle me. My reflexes are obviously also out of shape.

"Chad, have you made space in the storeroom for the shipment of the dry goods? It will be arriving any moment now."

Chad pounds his chest one last time and clears his throat while shaking his head. "I was just about to do that," he says in a wheezy voice.

"Wonderful. Merci."

Jean-Pierre looks at me, his gaze saying, "Your time is up."

I nod, thank Chad, and leave him one of my cards. He glances at it before depositing it into his baggy jeans pocket.

"If you think of anything else, please get in touch."

He smiles at me, slow and crooked. "Sure," he says.

Chapter Five

I run a few errands on foot, the sun slowly warming the air until, finally, it's bearable to breathe. The walking, too, is warming me up. Feeling inspired, I decide to continue to the state police barracks. I'll ask C.J. about the missing person's report rather than call him.

Crossing Main Street, the smell of onions and fresh seafood wafting from a nearby restaurant make me alternately hungry and nauseous. One of the meds I'm taking upsets my stomach early in the day. My feet make little powdery puffs with each step. The sidewalks are cracked and broken in spots and I go slowly enough that I can map out my next several steps before taking them. Between being careful not to fall, my medication's side effects, and stretchy pants, I've become an old lady.

My heart pounds toward the top of the hill, reminding me how out of shape I am, my breath coming in fast, steamy clouds. Sweat has broken out on my forehead. My shoulder area is aching and I long to stick a hand under my coat and shirt and rub the spot.

Instead, I distract myself. What was Chad going to say about Sandra? He knows her, obviously, but his reaction wasn't what I'd expected. Unless he's the one dating her? That would explain the choking. I try to picture the two of them as a couple. I've seen stranger things, though height-wise she'd tower over him. I'd guess he's about five-seven at the most and she's got to be closer to six feet.

Finally, blissfully, the road begins to level off. I walk past a new housing development where large houses line a semi-private drive, then, the site of the Governor Smith mansion which, supposedly, is haunted. I don't get any weird vibes passing by it, though. The place looks beautiful, as always. A handful of older homes line the next portion of the street before turning to newer houses. I pass Hard'ack, a place for downhill skiing, snowboarding, and sledding in winter and where I run sprints in summer. Ten minutes later I'm at the state police barracks parking lot. A dark green cruiser pulls in and slows.

I glance over and see a familiar tall, straight form in the driver's seat.

"Hey, this is a nice surprise," C.J. says as the window glides down. "What are you doing here?"

"Looking for you."

C.J. grins.

"I need to grab something from my desk before heading into the city. I'm due at the courthouse. Want to ride along?"

"Sure," I say.

"Hop in."

I open the passenger door and slide in, the interior warm and welcoming. C.J. jogs to the glass door and goes inside the building. The car smells spicy, like C.J.'s cologne. Buttons and a tiny laptop and all sorts of other technical things I don't recognize line the dash. I sink into the passenger seat with a little sigh.

"Feeling okay?" C.J. asks moments later, tucking paperwork into the console between us and pulling out of the lot.

"Fine. Just old and fat and tired."

C.J. makes a "hmm" sound. If you're looking for reassurances, don't look to C.J. He's the worst pep-talk-giver I've ever met.

"How's your PT going?" He turns out of the parking area and onto Route 105.

I shrug my shoulders. "Good, I guess. I'm not making the progress I'd hoped. My shoulder still aches a lot with any activity. Not that I've even made it to the gym lately."

"You should come to work out with me sometime."

C.J.'s workouts take place late at night when I'm pulling on jammies and snuggling into bed. There's nothing I look forward to less after a long day of work than going to the gym. I look at him. His eyes are focused on me instead of the road. He gives me a slow smile and turns his attention back to the wheel.

We're still new at this we-used-to-date-but-now-are-just-friends thing. Is it always going to feel this awkward? It's like we're having one conversation out loud but another one is going on below the surface. Or is it just my imagination?

"I stopped by because I was looking for some information on a new client," I say.

"Oh." Even *I'm* not so socially out of touch that I miss the disappointment in his voice. "It's a working visit, then," he says.

I nod, deciding to play dumb and avoid a potentially uncomfortable conversation.

"A woman in town called me to track down her missing

boyfriend. You know her family, probably. They own Garrison's Gym." C.J.'s fingers slip on the steering wheel suddenly and he clears his throat, replanting them.

"She said she filed a police report but that not a lot had been done," I say. "I just wanted to double-check, see what was going on."

C.J. nods. Curt. Quick. "What's the guy's name?"

I tell him.

"Doesn't ring a bell. I can check when I get back to the barracks and see." He pauses and rubs a hand over his cheek. His fingers are long. He would have made an excellent piano player.

"I appreciate it," I say.

We ride the rest of the way into town in silence. It's not a comfortable one, though, and I try to think of something to talk about.

"How's work going?" I finally manage. Not my most original conversation starter, but hey, I've done worse.

"Busy, as always. Got a couple of recruits starting at the end of this week."

"Anyone you'll be overseeing?"

C.J. shakes his head. "Not that I know of."

Another couple minutes of quiet and then I ask if he can drop me off at my office before heading to the courthouse.

"That's where I was headed," he says tightly.

"Oh."

"Look, Tayt—" he starts.

At the same time, I say, "C.J., I really—"

We glance at each other and laugh. For a second it's like it used to be. Fences down, familiarity in the look. But then I turn to look at my hands, rubbing my fingers together. My skin is dry and the sound makes a small *scritch, scritch* sound.

C.J. clears his throat and begins again. "I was just going to say that, uh, I was wondering if you'd want to get dinner sometime this weekend."

The only sound between us is the wheels humming. Occasionally, one of the tires hits a snow clot and crunches.

"I can't," I say. "I have a security detail this weekend and I don't think—"

"Security detail. Already?" He cranes in his seat to look at me, his eyes going automatically to my shoulder. "Are you sure you're up to it?"

My breath comes out in a whoosh. "You sound like my mother."

"I just think you should take it easy. You just said that your PT isn't going well. Anyway, someone has to look out for you. It might as well be me." He says this with absolute certainty. His attention is back on the road.

Heat fills my cheeks. This time it's not from embarrassment.

This isn't going to work. The words bang around in my head, not for the first time in recent months. I can't do this post-breakup-friendship stuff. I can't deal with C.J. and his possessiveness. It's not just now—it's what it reminds me of. He's always acted like he knew what I needed better than me. He has no claim, I remind myself, especially after the way our relationship ended years ago.

"Look, I don't need you or anyone else to look out for me, okay? I've got it covered." The words were supposed to sound light and jokey but instead are closer to a snarl. C.J. glances at me again, surprise marring his perfectly handsome face. Sometimes I hate him for being so attractive.

"Can you just let me out here?" I ask, hand on the door

handle.

"No, I can't," C.J. says. "This is an unsafe area to get out of a vehicle."

I roll my eyes in response.

He slows down moments later, applies the blinker, and pulls over. Then he turns and looks at me. I don't make eye contact. I start to feel hot and itchy, like a pure wool sweater is covering my bare flesh.

"What is going on with you?" C.J. asks. "Why the hostility? I thought we were supposed to be friends. You know *friends*." He draws the word out as though it has many syllables. He sighs and stares out of the windshield, his long arms hanging over the steering wheel. "I'm just looking out for you, you know."

Awkward pause.

"I know you are," I say. "And I didn't mean to sound… ungrateful. It's just that it's been months now of my mother and everyone else checking on me and asking how I'm feeling and telling me what I should and shouldn't be doing to get better. I appreciate the concern, but honestly?" Both of my hands rise and then fall to my lap limply. "It's exhausting. And frustrating. I know how to take care of myself. I'm following the doctor's orders"—(*okay, this is a small lie*)—"I don't need an army of people telling me what to do."

"Big surprise there." C.J. has a smile on his face. I can tell, even though I'm not looking at him. Part of me wants to shake him hard enough to make the smile fall off and another part of me wants to curl up against his chest and let him take care of me.

"I'd better go. I have a lot of work to do still."

My fingers are already gripping the lever to open it when

he says, "You know we're just concerned about you, Tayt. It's not a bad thing to have people care about you."

But I feel like I'm being strangled. I keep the words trapped behind my teeth.

"I know," I say instead. "Thanks for the ride."

"Anytime," C.J. says and grabs my hand across the seat.

It's warm and softer than you'd expect.

"Really, Tayt. You know that I'm here for you anytime, right?"

I nod, try to smile, then squeeze his fingers and let his hand fall, closing the door quietly.

****

I spend the afternoon puttering about in my office, filling out paperwork and filing it, and updating the website. After a brief nap at my desk, I rub creases from my left cheek and try calling Reba using the burner phone. There is no answer and I decide not to leave a message.

Chewing the inside of my lip, I think about the messages she'd left. Her voice had sounded so worried—desperate, almost. I make a mental note to try her again later today.

I open the file for the security gig in Colchester. It's in three days and I haven't set anything up yet. I make a note of the address. A house party, the musician's mother had said. I MapQuest it, then print out the map and make a few notes. I'll do a drive-by, maybe stop in and ask the owners if I can take a look around inside. I'm assuming the party will be indoors since it's the middle of winter.

The group should be small, less than thirty people. Party-goers in their mid-twenties, though, so definitely an alcohol-focused crowd—drugs likely, too. Generally, I'd need backup. A crowd this size at a private function can be handled by one security guard or bouncer, but it's better with two. Plus, I'm not playing my A-game. I don't want to fork over a chunk of the payment, though. I need the cash too much at this point.

I yawn and stretch. As good as it feels to get caught up on paperwork, the inactivity leaves me sleepy and lazy. How do people who have desk jobs do it? I'd weigh at least another hundred pounds and be as mobile as a sloth in my off-hours.

Closing down the computer, I grab my bag and make sure the coffee pot is off, then head to the parking area. I've got time to check out the house in Colchester and maybe, if I'm lucky, make it to the gym before dinner.

Chapter Six

It's Friday night and the house party/concert I'm working at begins in just over an hour. Nausea sets in and this time it's not medicine-related.

I am going to fail tonight.

If anything happens—if a guest is drunk and it gets out of hand—I will fail. I can't do this. What was I thinking? My breath comes quick and short in my chest and my throat feels as narrow as a plastic drinking straw. The edges of my vision become gray. I want to laugh, thinking how ridiculous I must look right now. But there's no air for laughter, or anything else.

I put my head between my legs and force my body to take one slow, deep breath, then another. The breathing sounds ragged in my ears (which are buzzing slightly).

I continue. *In. Out. In. Out.*

The phone rings and it startles me so much that I jerk upward, banging my head against the bottom of the kitchen table. I rub the spot while reaching for the phone and see that it's C.J. Am I ready for another lecture?

Breathe. *In. Out. In. Out.* Maybe it will calm me down.

"Hello?" I try to make the word sound as normal as possible.

It sounds tinny and small. I clear my throat and am about to try again when C.J. starts talking.

"Hey, it's me. I wanted to tell you that I looked into your missing person."

I hear papers moving and picture C.J.'s fingers shuffling through them.

"There's nothing here," he says. "I've been through the reports and there hasn't been one filed by Sandra Garrison or anyone else for Mark Chester."

That doesn't make sense. I chew my lip, thinking. "Are you sure?" I ask finally.

"Positive."

"That's weird." Why would she lie about filing a report with the police? "Thanks for checking for me. I appreciate it." Had I told C.J. Sandra's name or just asked if a report had been filed? Garrison's is a pretty popular gym. Maybe he knows Sandra from there and put two and two together.

"No problem," C.J.'s voice cuts in. "You can pay me back by meeting me for a drink in about an hour. Or dinner, if that's better." His voice is sure, confident. Bossy. The skin on my neck crinkles and I scratch it, still working on normal breathing.

"I've got that security job in Colchester tonight, remember? Gotta run," I say and hang up before he can start lecturing.

Straightening to my full height, I walk into the bathroom where I'd been getting ready before the breathing issue started. "Breathing issue" sounds much better than hyperventilation.

Makeup is spread around the sink and my hairdryer is right where I left it, dangling from the outlet by the curly cord. I disconnect it, rewind the cord around the unit, and put it away. I finish curling my eyelashes and apply a quick coat of mascara, all the time reminding myself that this is a low-key party, that I could do this job with a hand tied behind my back.

Yeah, before the accident, that nasty little voice reminds me.

I dump the makeup back into the bag a little harder than I need to. The voice has gotten louder in these last two months than it's ever been before.

"You're finding that your confidence is shaken, now that you've had this serious injury," I picture my therapist telling me. I haven't been to see her in weeks.

Maybe you should schedule an appointment, the voice says. *Maybe that's why you're having panic attacks in the bathroom.*

I force myself to relax as I double-check my appearance. I don't look scared and overwhelmed like someone who needs a paper bag to keep from having a nervous breakdown. My new black dress pants, two sizes larger than I usually wear, hide most of my girth. My *T.R. Waters Securities* black, collared shirt is tucked into the waistband, showcasing a utility belt filled with security options: Handcuffs, pepper spray, and my newest addition—a tightly bound, carbon fiber rod about eight inches in length that unfurls to three feet. It's virtually unbendable and unbreakable. It can crack a man's bone with one forceful hit.

"I won't need any of them," I tell the empty room. "Everything is going to be fine. This is an easy gig."

Forty minutes later I pull into the driveway. It's long and narrow, covered in pea stone, and crunches under the car's tires. There is hardly any snow here at all, just a light dusting on the lawn. The house appears after a bend shrouded with trees. It's beautiful—a modern farmhouse, ready to have its picture taken for a glossy home decorating magazine. A wide porch wraps around the house and is filled with people milling about. Small fires burning in filigreed fire pots flicker near the porch. I get out of the car and walk toward the rear door, winding my way through BMWs and Lexus sedans and a few enormous SUVs. Laughter and the sound of ice clinking in glasses float across the air to me. The band hasn't started playing yet.

No one answers my knock, so I let myself in. The house is as immaculate as when I visited the first time, with soaring cathedral ceilings and white on nearly every surface. It's a strange effect, as though I'm walking into a glass of milk.

Julia is a middle-aged woman, plump and well-dressed. She scurries by and I clear my throat.

"Hello, Mrs. Lawson."

She jumps, startled.

"I'm sorry, no one answered my knock," I say.

"Oh, my dear, I'm sorry, I didn't hear the door? My son and his friends decided it was too beautiful a night to stay indoors?" Again with the high notes turning every sentence into a question. I grit my teeth and paste a big, fat smile on my face.

"You can come right through here?"

I follow Julia Lawson through the house and then through a side door, ending up near the edge of the wide front lawn. She introduces me to the band, a three-piece funk-jazz-rock ensemble in which her son, Alexander, plays drums. I smile, nod, and shake hands all around.

The crowd is relaxed and though the music hasn't officially started, the drinking has. Still, I can hardly picture a mosh pit sprouting up on the lawn anytime soon. I walk the perimeter, using my Mag flashlight to check the area hidden by brush, then plant myself at the side and front of the crowd. I'm near enough that people can see the back of my windbreaker which reads "security" in wide white letters, but not in the way that blocks their view of the band. My breath forms in white clouds but just barely, the temperature more like a cool spring night than a frigid mid-January one.

The band starts about twenty minutes later. The music isn't bad and the food looks delicious, catered by a company out of Burlington. I have a rule that I don't eat or drink on the job, though my mouth waters when I make another round near the food table. As the night goes on, the crowd disperses onto the lawn, dancing and shimmying to the beat. Woolen hats fly from heads and jackets are shed as the group dances. Yells from happy fans become background vocals to the music when a particularly popular song is played.

I listen and watch. Watch and listen.

My cellphone reads midnight when the hair on my neck stands up. I heard something. A noise I can't quite place. But what?

I check the crowd. Dancing bodies, many pressed together in a rendition of Patrick Swayze and Jennifer Gray's moves in *Dirty Dancing*, crowd the center of the lawn. The music is still loud, the amps pouring out heavy bass and percussion, while one of the singers strums his guitar and croons. I clear my head of all these sounds while I listen for something else.

There it is again. A thready meow of pain. Definitely human. I walk in the direction of the parking area, pause, and wait. The next time I hear the sound it's quieter and coming from the woods near the driveway. I scan the crowd again, part of me wishing that I'd asked C.J. to play backup, part of me tingling with anticipation. I walk to the edge of the wooded area, drawing out the powerful flashlight but not flicking it on.

The light from a nearly full moon illuminates my path into the trees for a few seconds, but then branches crowd it out. If I switch the light on, I'll get a better view, but it will also notify whoever's out there of my presence. Silence is hard to maintain on the newly bare ground. Wet leaves, twigs, and smashed-down grass line the way. There's noise to my right, a shuffling of something and snapping branches. I change course slightly and head in that direction, moving as quietly as I can. Switching the flashlight to my left hand, I pull out the night stick and hold my breath. My feet move closer to the sound. My heart beats hard in my chest.

There! Another small gasp of pain. I lunge through the remaining feet, hand drawn high overhead with the stick, ready to crack it down on someone's head. A young woman stands against a tree, her dress up around her waist. A guy in his twenties, long-haired and rumpled, stands in front of her. His pants around his ankles, his buttocks white in the moonlight that's reappeared.

"Get away from her," I say, my voice steely in the chilly night air.

The woman screams. The man whirls toward me.

Chapter Seven

"Did you hear me? I said get away from her—now—or I'll knock you into the next county."

The woman bends forward, hands pulling her dress down. My brain is already planning out the next steps: Handcuff the guy, call 9-1-1, practice some roundhouse kicks on his shaggy head while waiting for the cops and ambulance to get here.

The man just stands there, facing me, arms loose by his sides. His eyes, I can see in the abrasive flashlight beam, are half-shut. I lower the night stick by several inches.

"Put your clothes on," I say. "You picked the wrong party to have a date rape."

"What?" Both voices speak in unison.

"Date rape?" The woman's head reappears after pulling her undies up from around her ankles. She is tall and thin, her legs tanned even in the moonlight.

"No way," the man says in a far-out-this-is-trippy kind of way.

"You've got it all wrong," the woman says, and I can see a wide smile on her face. Laughter tumbles out between her words.

"I wasn't being raped. We were…do I have to spell it out for you?" She motions with her hand. "We came here with other people but sort of got together on the dance floor."

The man nods along as the woman speaks.

"We were looking for a little, you know, privacy?" she says, stretching out the last word.

You've got to be joking.

I lower the night stick the rest of the way while they huddle close together. Pot=head guy has pulled up his baggy cargo pants, and says, "Hey, we're not, like, under arrest or anything, are we?"

I shake my head and turn around, ready to rejoin the party and see if anything wild and crazy has happened in my absence.

"Could we borrow your handcuffs anyway?" he asks as I walk away. Her laughter tumbles behind me.

The party finishes up after one-thirty and I collect the rest of my wages from Mrs. Lawson. I assured her that she could send a check to the office but in her strange, questioning voice she told me, "Really? Let's take care of everything tonight."

I could use the money, so I don't argue.

I wait until most of the guests clear out, then find my car. The air is thick with smoke, some from the fire burners and some from cannabis that was discreetly smoked in the makeshift parking area. I see the hippie chick from the woods holding hands with the guy she must have come with. They are polar opposites; he looks like an investment banker, preppy with his hair neatly trimmed. She leads him to an older model Saab and glances at me over her shoulder. She puts a finger to her lips playfully and gives me a wink. I roll my eyes and get in my car, then drive home and collapse into bed. My shoulder aches, but I smile in the darkness. It feels good to be back in the saddle.

***

Saturday morning dawns clear but cold. The weatherman had predicted that the spring-like temperatures wouldn't be long-lasting and he was right. I went for a walk after my first cup of coffee, feeling a little less like an old woman than usual. Maybe the boost in self-esteem was affecting my health, too.

When I get back, sweaty and panting slightly after climbing the hill near the trailer, I check for messages (none), swig a big glass of water, and make some toast. I look longingly at the coffee pot but figure that if I am going to clean up my act health-wise, I should probably limit my consumption to a couple of cups a day. Maybe I should try making one of those smoothies like I had at Juice Bar. Thinking of it reminds me that I need to call Sandra. I dial her cell phone. No answer. Next, I try the gym.

"Garrison's Gym, this is Sandra." Her voice is annoyingly perky so early in the morning. I glance at the clock. *Oh, well.* Still, too perky for eleven o'clock.

"Hi, Sandra, it's Tayt. I have a couple of questions for you. Can I meet you when you get done with work?"

Pause.

"Sure," she breathes out, her voice quieter. "I'm done in an hour, if that works. I had the early morning shift. Do you want to meet at Juice Bar again or somewhere else?"

"I'm just getting ready to go in to work myself. Can you meet me at my office?"

She agrees, so I give her the address and we hang up. I take a quick shower, do a few PT stretches between shampooing my hair and shaving my legs, and make it to the office moments before she arrives.

Sandra seems even taller in the low-ceilinged space. Today she's wearing some kind of snug Lycra pants and a hot pink coat trimmed with fur. I motion to a seat near my desk and ask if she wants coffee. If she wanted some, maybe I could have a small cup.

"No, thanks," she says, quashing that dream. "What's this about? Did you find something out about Mark?"

I chew the inside of my cheek for a moment. How to do this tactfully? Not that I haven't been thinking about a way to handle this on my twenty-minute commute to St. Albans.

Perhaps bluntness is best. "Why don't you tell me why you lied about filing a police report?" I ask.

Sandra starts to form the word "what" on her lips, but when I lower my chin and give her my don't-even-try-it glare, she instead looks at the ceiling. Then her hands.

"I don't know what you're talking about. I most certainly did go down to the police barracks and file paperwork. Maybe they've lost it," she says finally.

I shake my head. "That's not possible. Sandra, the police don't just lose paperwork. Besides, I have a friend on the force."

Her head snaps back to front and center and she stares at me.

"He searched all their missing person reports. You never filed it. Why not? And why tell me that you did?"

Sandra looks away out the window and then rises from her seat and walks to it. The panes of glass are smeared with dust. When she turns back toward me seconds later, tears are making their way down her face.

"You got me, okay? I didn't file the report. I did go to the station, but I got too scared in the parking lot and ended up just leaving. I thought…" She breaks off and motions to the box of tissues on my desk.

I hand them to her. Stretching causes a little shiver of pain in my shoulder and chest.

"I thought you wouldn't want to start looking unless everything had been done all legally. I needed to find Mark and I didn't want to get the police involved in case he wasn't missing. I mean, imagine trying to explain to him if the police picked him up somewhere."

"But he is missing, isn't he? Why would you need to explain your worry to the police when Mark's been missing several days? That seems like a pretty normal concern for his girlfriend to have."

Sandra blows her nose and gives me a smile that wavers.

"I just…got scared. And now I'm scared on two levels. I'm afraid to get the police involved in case this is completely innocent and I'm scared to not involve them because something bad may have happened to Mark."

"So that's why you called me."

Sandra nods slowly. She looks like she's about to say something else, but looks out of the window again instead.

"Have you found anything yet?" she asks.

I shake my head. "No. I'm going to talk to his friend, Chad, again. Is there anyone else—any other friends?"

"Chad from the restaurant?" she asks.

I nod.

Sandra makes a noise that sounds disgusted and shakes her head. "Don't believe a word he says. The guy's been in jail on drug charges more than once. He's a complete waste of breath."

"Well, at this point I don't have a lot of other avenues to try. I've spoken with his boss, who knows nothing. You're telling me he has no other friends, no family in the area. How far are you willing to go with this? Should I book a plane ticket to his childhood home and start checking with his relatives there?"

Sandra nods.

"And you won't consider filing a report officially? I encourage you to do that, Sandra. It would be a lot easier if we had the resources that the police can offer—"

"No. Please, not yet. I will if it comes to that, but for now, I just want you to do what you can, okay?"

I look at her, eyes unwavering. She's stopped crying, but her eyes plead with me. "Whatever it takes. I can pay you whatever is needed. I just want to find out what's happened to him." Her eyes tear up again and she presses the tissue over them.

***

Despite Sandra's claims that Chad is a convicted felon and not to be trusted, I stop by the restaurant to talk to him again. He's not there. One of the waitstaff tells me it's his day off and that I might find him at the gym or the billiards hall.

I try the billiards hall first. It's a retro-looking place on Kingman Street, its décor is nostalgic: old black and white photos of St. Albans city back in the 50s, kids walking to school with hobo-style lunches carried on sticks, old trains crisscrossing city streets. Red carpet lines the floor. There are four pool tables set up in a large rectangle, and near the back a group of men and a single woman play darts.

Chad is playing by himself at the table in the far corner. A lone beer bottle sits on the side of the green-carpeted table.

"Hi, remember me?" I ask.

He looks up from the shot, pauses, looks back down, and connects the cue to the ball. It makes a satisfying smack and plunges a striped ball into the pocket nearest me.

"Sure, how're you doing?" he says. He doesn't sound enthusiastic, but not quite aloof, either.

I nod. "Listen, I don't want to be a pest, but I had a couple more questions for you. About Mark."

Chad stands to his full height, shakes dreads out of his eyes, and sips from the bottle of Long Trail.

"I don't know what else I can tell you. I don't know where he is. Still haven't heard from him."

I nod. "I was wondering about Mark's relationship with Sandra. How well do you know her?"

Chad chokes a little on his swallow of beer.

"Okay," I say. "That's the second time you've choked, literally, when I brought up her name."

"Sandra Garrison?" he asks, wiping the back of a hand over his mouth.

I nod again. He calls her a name I haven't heard since seventh-grade gym class.

"Can you expound on that a little?" I ask.

Chad smiles at me and sets his bottle on the side of the table.

"Sandra thinks that the world revolves around her. We were in school together and all through it she was the best in everything—sports, schoolwork, and drama club. She always had to be front and center. And if she wasn't, well, it wasn't pretty."

"What do you mean?"

Chad is silent for a minute, staring out toward the street. The group playing darts groans collectively, then one of the men slaps another on the back. The woman yells something I don't hear and a few guys laugh.

Chad takes another swig of beer, then watches me over the top of his bottle. His eyes rove from my face to feet and back again, but not in a way that feels overtly creepy. Rather, it's flattering. Or am I just so desperate for attention that I'm finding it that way?

His voice interrupts my thoughts, thankfully.

"Once she hired the school bully to beat up a kid who she thought was harassing her. He was a little, skinny dude and had a crush on her. Sandra didn't like it, she thought it ruined her image. So she paid this guy to beat the crap out of this kid after school.

"Another time, one of her competitors for the role in a school play broke her arm in a school skiing accident. There were rumors, you know. She just *happened* to have an accident after the tryout results were posted."

"Sandra didn't have the lead role?"

Chad shakes his head. "Nope. For the first time in all our four years of high school, someone else had gotten it. But not for long. She ended up being recast as the lead. Big surprise."

"People change," I say.

Chad shakes his head again, takes another pull from the bottle. "Not her."

"What about with Mark? She said they've been dating for only a short time. What did he think about her?"

Chad takes another swallow of beer. "Mark and Sandra? No, uh-uh. They weren't dating."

Pause.

"Why didn't you mention this to me before?" I ask. "Anyway, it's possible they were without your knowing."

"No way. Mark thought she was nuts. He was seriously considering moving to another gym just so he wouldn't have to see her. Said she was stalking him."

"He told you that?" I ask.

"Well, he was joking. But I wonder—"

"If he was serious?"

"I was going to say that I wonder if he left town because of it. Seems a little extreme, though."

I chew the inside of my cheek again, wondering what Sandra's deal is. And what about what she'd said about Chad? A convicted drug dealer—if that was true, how reliable was what he was telling me now? If I could just get a better feel for Mark as a person…

An idea springs to mind faster than a cat on a field mouse.

"I'll let you get back to your game," I say to Chad. "Thanks for talking with me. And please, give me a call if you hear anything from Mark, okay?"

"Sure," Chad says. He gives me a slow grin and turns back to the pool table.

I wonder if he will or if he's just trying to get rid of me.

"Do you play?" he calls over his shoulder while lining up a shot.

"Pool? No, not really."

"If you ever want to learn, I'm here most Tuesday and Thursday nights. Stop in sometime."

I glance back over my shoulder. "Thanks," I say. "I'll keep it in mind."

He gives me a nod and a wolfish smile as another ball smacks satisfyingly. Is he flirting with me? Stepping out of the door, a blast of icy air shakes the smile from my face. I hunker my shoulders down into my coat. I need to get into Mark's apartment.

If I can't trust Sandra…Or maybe she *is* the one I can trust, and it's Chad who's lying. Either way, I need to know who is telling the truth.

Breaking and entering is a crime. If I were a private investigator, I'd lose my license.

Good thing I'm not.

Chapter Eight

Mark Chester lives in an apartment house that's big and white and at one point was probably a single-family home. Like most of the houses in this area of the city, it has been converted into multiple apartment units. I park a block away and walk.

According to the information from Sandra, Mark lives in number four. The front door to the building is unlocked and leads to a dim hallway, a stairway on the right. Small mailboxes line the hallway wall, one for each of the four units. Since units one and two are on the lower level, I take the stairs. Number four is at the end of another short hallway, unfortunately directly across from unit three, where I can hear the faint strains of a game show through the door.

Should I knock on Mark's door? Chances are, he hasn't been hiding out in there for a week. Still, how awkward will it be if I jimmy the lock only to find him surfing the internet on a laptop in his underwear?

Despite my unease, I decide to try to open the door on my own. A knock will only notify the next-door neighbor that someone is out here; something I'd rather not do. I check the doorknob. It's old, brown, and round, maybe made of metal or even ceramic. There is a deadbolt above it. Scratch that. There are three deadbolts above the knob. Either Mark is scared of someone, or he's dealing drugs.

I try the old "credit card in the latch" trick three times with no positive results. The last time I try, my card bends so far I'm afraid it will snap and I'll leave evidence of my visit lodged in his door. I pull out my little lockpicking kit. I've just gotten the first tool into the first lock when my cell phone rings shrilly. I gasp, nearly dropping the entire kit on the ground. Glancing at the door nearby, I grab my stuff and hightail it back down the stairs as quietly as I can. I glance at the upper floor window as I answer the phone. A curtain moves, and then a white-haired lady peeks out. I duck behind a privacy hedge and follow it along the rear of the neighbor's property.

"Hello," my voice is irritated when I answer.

"Hello? This is Reba."

Reba. Reba. My brain whirls and I try to pull my thoughts back to the present, shaking off images of lock picking. Reba. The woman from the Sunflower Special phone. I yank the cellphone away from my ear. I must have grabbed both of them when I left the office.

"Yes, uh-huh. How can I help?" I say, walking back toward my car.

"I can't talk about it now, not over the phone," she says. "Can you meet me somewhere private? Two hours and come alone, okay?"

"Well, I'm sort of in the middle of—"

"Please," there is a gasp at the end of the word, like a prayer. "Meet me at the bike path, you know it? I'll be on a bench near mile thirteen marker. Please."

I look longingly back at the apartment building, doing some

quick math in my head.

"You'll come?" she repeats. "I'm desperate, please."

"Fine, yes, I'll be there."

"Thank you."

She ends the call without saying goodbye, so I stand there for a minute, phone pressed against my ear. I'm gnawing on the inside of my cheek again, a bad habit I'm trying to quit. I give myself a mental shake. My stomach growls. No wonder I'm nibbling, I think, and head back to my car.

Back at my office, I dig a dark wig and my theater makeup set out of the closet. Sunflower Specials require a different look, something to camouflage me from my real life. Imagine how awkward it would be to show up to meet a client for the first time and realize it's a friend of my mom's or an old grade-school teacher? I want to go no-fuss today, so I use the makeup sparingly, adding just enough shadows and fake moles to age me. I tug the wig into place and grin at myself. Yikes. I look like a blend of Cruella Deville and the Wicked Witch of the West.

Next, I drive up to Main Street and order a big smoothie and a couple of raw crepes from a perky blond girl at Juice Bar. I don't know about all this healthy eating. My head hurts. I'm hungry all the time. Or, rather, I'm craving deep-fried foods, meat, and chips all the time, which gives me a headache. Or maybe it's caffeine withdrawal? Whatever it is, it's not making my life happier.

Drinking the smoothie, I wait for my main dish. It comes a few minutes later, some brownish-looking things filled with strawberries and blueberries and drizzled with a sort of whipped cream and chocolate sauce. They don't look too bad. I push away the image of a Magic Moose sub from Big

Daddy's Deli Delight and try a forkful of the fruity concoction. It's pretty good. Inhaling the rest of my lunch, I polish off the smoothie and smile thanks at Perky Girl while depositing my dishes into a gray busboy bin. The makeup pulls at my cheeks. I check my watch. I have forty minutes to get to the Rail Trail spot.

I get there early and park in an area designated for visitors of the Rail Trail. Formerly a railroad line, it was converted into a walking/biking path years ago. It's lined with crushed stone and follows some of the prettiest countryside in Franklin County. Motorized vehicles aren't allowed, except this time of the year when it's used by snowmobilers. There won't be any out today, though, as just a light dusting of snow barely covers the ground.

The air is sharp and cold when I get out of the car. Grabbing a woolen hat from the back seat, I push it down on my head, mashing the curls of the wig slightly. I check my appearance one more time in the side mirror before heading off down the trail. How embarrassing would it be if one of my moles were falling off?

I like the sound my boots make on the half-frozen gravel. Other than that, the only thing I hear is the *caw-caw-caw* of a pair of crows in a nearby field and the quieter chatter of chickadees in the bare branches of a tree overhead. The air smells like winter, a mix of snow, pine, and other earthy things hibernating.

There is a figure on the bench as I approach the marker for mile thirteen. I walk as though I have a purpose, like I'm one of those people out getting my daily dose of fresh air and multiplying endorphins. As I get closer, I see that it's a woman sitting on the bench. She has pale skin and eyes. I'd guess she's in her mid-thirties, small and round.

"Hello," I say, slowing. "Are you Reba?"

"Yes. Thank you for coming."She pats the bench next to her.

"Do you mind if we walk?" I ask. "We'll stay warmer."

She nods, points away from the direction I just came.

We fall in step; Reba's legs aren't much shorter than mine. I can smell wood smoke and another scent that I can't place coming off of her clothes.

"I'm sorry that it took so long to get ahold of me," I say. "It's been really busy."

Plus, I'm a bit of a coward. I clear my throat. "So, you said that your daughter was in some sort of trouble?"

Reba nods. "Leanne. My daughter's thirteen. She…" The woman's voice fades out for a minute. A tiny chickadee in a tree nearby says, *Chick-a-dee-dee-dee.* "She's a good girl; she never causes trouble, my Leanne. Good grades in school, well-behaved girl."

I wait for the "but" like a bad punchline. *But she's pregnant and we want you to kill the father. But she started using drugs. But she ran away to become an actress and ended up on the streets.*

"We work on a farm in Enosburg, it's a big place. More than three hundred head of cow. My husband and me work in the barn during the day while the kids are in school, you know? We have three kids, Leanne, and two younger boys. Leanne started working for the farmer, in the house. She works after school until dinner time. But now…" Reba pauses again and when I glance over, she's biting her lip, tears welling in her eyes. "Now I'm scared. I don't want her to go there anymore."

"Why not?" I ask, though a sinking feeling in my gut tells me I already know.

"The farmer—he's a good man. Well-known, community

guy, you know? But I think he likes her too much. At first, he told us that she was like a daughter to him—he never had a daughter. But that's not how he looks at her. Last week, I went to the house even though we're not supposed to. There was a problem with the pipes in the barn that bring water to the cows. I knocked but no one answered. I went inside.

"The farmer, he had his hands on Leanne. He had pushed her up against the wall and was trying to touch her. She was fighting him and when she saw me, she started to cry. He turned around and his face got real still. Then he told me to get out. I said, 'No, not without Leanne.' Then he got real red. He was so mad he was shaking. He walked to the barn, so fast we couldn't keep up. And then he threatened my husband, told him we'd all lose our jobs if he caught me at the house again. Said I misunderstood, didn't see what I thought I had."

"What did your husband say?"

She shrugs, looks toward the ground. "Not much. He said I shouldn't rock the boat, should mind my own business."

"Even after you told him what the farmer was doing to Leanne?" The hair on the back of my neck is standing up.

"My husband…he was mad—really angry, you know? But he said that we can't risk it."

I stop walking.

"I'm sorry. You lost me here. He doesn't think that letting his daughter get assaulted by his boss is a risk?"

"No. I mean, yes. But my husband can't…he can't help. And then he feels mad, so he tells me to mind my own business. He loves Leanne, he does. But he's scared, too, you know?"

Wheels in my brain have been churning and finally spit something out that makes sense.

"Because you're not working at the farm legally."

Reba nods.

We start walking again, Reba extracting a tissue from her jacket and wiping at her eyes, her running nose.

"My husband's been in jail. Federal prison. He served his time, but no one will hire an ex-con. He was out of work for more than a year after he got released. I worked as a waitress but it wasn't enough to make ends meet. Plus, we were already in hot water because I couldn't keep up with all the bills while he was in the pen. Farming is what he grew up doing, so he went back to it. But the farmer doesn't want anyone to know that my husband works there; he thinks it would be bad for his reputation. So, he pays us under the table. We get housing—if you can call it that—and cash. It's just for now."

"Well, the farmer—you never told me his name," I say.

"It is Emerson. Emerson Prescott."

I nearly trip over a root poking out of the hard gravel.

"Emerson Prescott?" I sound like a parrot. Reba doesn't seem to notice and just nods in agreement.

Holy crap. Are you kidding me? is what I want to say. Instead, I murmur a sound that hopefully comes off as a positive acknowledgment. Why didn't I think to ask Reba who this man was before now? Why do I always forget seemingly small details which turn into mountainous problems?

The Prescotts have been farming the fields in Franklin County for years. No, scratch that, centuries. They are well-known because they are successful at it. No matter what hit the other farms take every year—hailstorms or drought, an infestation of locusts, for pity's sake—the Prescotts remain seemingly untouched.

On top of that, Emerson Prescott is known for his upstanding community involvement. He's worked with the various schools in the area, volunteers on more than one nonprofit board, and sponsors many fundraisers throughout the year. "Prescott Acres Farm" appears on banners in everything from the Enosburg Dairy Days to the St. Albans Maple Festival parade and many other events in between.

Crap.

Double crap.

I nearly blurt out, *Are you sure of what you saw?* and then realize how demoralizing that would be. Of course, Reba is sure. The stakes for her are high and the ferocity of a mother's love is like a bear's. I imagine what it must be like to see your adolescent daughter manhandled by your boss and landlord.

"I understand your situation, Reba, but how exactly could I help?" I ask gently.

She sighs and we turn and begin retracing our steps.

"My friend's friend told me about your Sunflower Specials. She said you helped her. We have some money saved up—I've been putting a little aside. My husband doesn't know I'm talking to you." Reba dabs at her eyes again. "I just want to keep Leanne safe. I want Mr. Prescott to leave her alone."

"Can't you just tell him that she's not allowed to work at the house anymore?"

"No. I talked to my husband and he talked to Mr. Prescott. He needs Leanne there, to help with housecleaning and some cooking. His wife left him maybe two months ago? I've been going with Leanne; he doesn't like it, but I told him it's the only way. The thing is that with chores, I can't always be up there at the same time she is. He said he needs help until he finds a housekeeper to come work full-time."

"And if you refuse to let Leanne go—"

"He says we'll lose our jobs, that we'll all be out on the street.

I told my husband we should call the police, but he refuses. No one will believe us over Prescott, that's what he says." She frowns. "He's probably right, least of all the cops."

I rub a hand over my forehead, then remember my makeup and let it drop back to my side.

"So, you want me to…hurt Prescott?"

"Not hurt, exactly," Reba says. "Just get him to leave Leanne alone."

And just how am I supposed to do that?

Chapter Nine

When I pull into the parking lot off Lake Street, the sun is nearly setting over the lake. The air is colder, the temperature dropping quickly. I'm thinking about Reba, Leanne, and Prescott as I hurry up the stairs and don't bother turning the light on. I've stopped by to grab the bills I'd paid but forgotten to put in the mail earlier. Tucking the small stack into my coat pocket, I turn to leave when the phone rings.

There is nothing like the sound of a ringing telephone or a screeching teakettle. Either sound says *deal with me now!* in a way that other noises can't. Answer it or let it go to voicemail? My skin tingles. Is it another creepy anonymous call?

I reach across the desk.

"T.R. Waters Securities, this is Tayt."

"Hey, it's me." Ezra's voice is warm and welcome and I perch on the edge of the vintage, green beast of a desk. Am I happier that it's my best friend or that it's not the creepy stalker? Hard to tell.

"I haven't heard from you in a while," he's saying. "Wondering if you might want to grab a cup of coffee and see a movie."

"I'm glad it's you. I didn't realize you were back in town." My fingers wind the curly cord of the phone's handle. "Sure, I'd love to. When were you thinking?"

"Whatever works for you. I'm free tonight and tomorrow night and then again on Friday." His voice changes slightly, dropping an octave. "How've you been feeling, by the way? Healing well?"

I grimace. Ezra is my oldest friend. Why does his concern rub me the wrong way? Why does everyone's worry irritate me so much?

"Fine. I'm good," I say breezily. "I have to run, I just stopped by to pick something up. Why didn't you call my cell?"

"I tried. Dead battery?"

I pull the phone from my pocket and see that the battery is spent. "Yup, you're right."

Ezra chuckles. "I usually am."

I roll my eyes, pocketing the phone. I'll have to charge it when I get home. My Toyota is too ancient to expel any extraordinary effort at this point.

"Tomorrow night is good," I say. "Want to meet at the theater?"

"Sure," Ezra says. "You can pick the movie, but it will have to be the early show. And please, Tayt, no chick flicks."

I laugh. He knows I hate them as much as he does—maybe even more. Although I'm pretty sure he hadn't disliked the one that we saw accidentally—it'd looked like an action movie—as much as he'd said he had. We decide on the time and place to meet and hang up.

***

I find the same parking place I'd used this morning on

High Street and get out, walking quickly in the cold to Mark's apartment building. Lights are on in both downstairs apartments, but the old woman's apartment across from Mark's is dark. That's good. Hopefully, granny is tucked in bed, snoozing away.

Opening the exterior door to the building, I quietly close it behind me. The stairs aren't particularly squeaky, but they *are* wood and I'd prefer not to notify everyone in the building that I'm here. I walk up as quietly as one can in thick winter boots. The smell of leftover dinner hangs above my head in the hall. Something greasy and meaty.

Extracting the small kit from my backpack, I kneel before Mark's door. There is no light on and no sound coming from behind the door. I hold a tiny flashlight in between my teeth and work at the locks. Success comes in mere seconds for the first deadbolt, then a bit longer for the second and third. While the landlord might not be overly concerned about safety, Mark sure is.

I put my tools away and slowly turn the knob. There's a loud creak as the door edges open and I stop and hold my breath. I listen, expecting the elderly neighbor's light to blind me or for the neighbors downstairs to pop their heads out and find out what the noise was. Neither happens. I wait another few seconds and then walk into the darkness, pushing the door closed behind me quickly.

Using the small penlight instead of turning on any lights, I get a lay of the land. Unfortunately, the beam is only meant for close up. It dissipates and fades just a few feet from where I'm standing.

Still, it casts enough illumination to map out the basics. I'm standing in the living room. There's an extra-long couch along one wall and across from it, a big flat-screen TV with speakers mounted on the wall. I walk further into the room. A weight bench with a lot of plates sits in front of the big windows. The blinds are up and the curtains are open. I'm glad I didn't turn on any lights. I turn to my right and nearly collide with a stack of CDs. While the nosy part of me wants to see what music Mark likes, I resist. I'm here to get information and get out, the faster the better.

Following the wall, I grope at the next doorway and enter a small kitchen. There are no dirty dishes in the sink and a quick peek in the fridge shows several half-full condiments and little else. Passing through the kitchen, I enter an open area with little in it. Maybe it's supposed to be a den or study. Off of this room are a bathroom and bedroom.

I look in the bathroom first. There are a few personal items: a pair of fingernail clippers, some washcloths and towels, and a nearly-gone stick of deodorant. The medicine cabinet holds various boxes and bottles of vitamins, ibuprofen, and other things that normally make their home in a medicine cabinet.

Frustrated, I move on to the bedroom. So far there is nothing in the apartment to suggest that there is anything suspicious about Mark missing. The bed is unmade (no crime there), drawers are mostly full of clothes, and the book shelf is nearly full. While I'd resisted my nosiness regarding the man's musical tastes, I cannot do the same regarding books. It's fascinating to see what people read. Mark's taste runs from paperback westerns to New Age philosophy to health books, particularly those featuring raw cooking. Or un-cooking, I guess. A few books are missing in this area.

There is no computer or tablet in the room, or anywhere else in the apartment that I've seen. A small table in the corner of the room looks like where he'd normally plug in. A pair of speakers and notebook and pen rest there, along with a dust outline of a rectangle the size of a laptop.

I flip through the notebook. There are notes about workout plans, a complicated diagram of weight versus height versus fitness exertion, and some scribbled notes about appointments. These quicken my heartbeat until I see that the date is from last year. I flip further forward in the notebook. Finally, on the second to last page, I see something useful. A note about a place called "West Fresh Institute" and a town that I've never heard of in Arizona.

I guess it's not unusual that I haven't heard of it, as I've never traveled out west. Once upon a time, I'd planned to live in L.A. or New York City. It feels like a lifetime ago, like the dreams of another person. I make a note of the institute and spend another couple of minutes poking around in the junk drawer in the kitchen and the living room side tables. There is nothing else of interest. A pile of bills tells me that Mark is up to date with his utilities and that he doesn't keep a balance on his credit card. I make a note of his landlord's name and address found on a contract in a shoebox in the living room. The man's filing system makes my own look impressive.

Carefully putting the paperwork back where I found it, I sigh. It wasn't a completely wasted trip, but I wish I'd found more. Suddenly, blue lights paint themselves across the room. I freeze, then drop to all fours.

Crappity crap.

The neighbor called the cops. I'm trapped.

Think! Think! Think!

I search my recent memory for potential hiding spots in the apartment. The kitchen cabinets are large, but I'm not sure they are quite large enough. Under the bed? In the closet? Hysterical laughter starts in my belly, but I squash it.

Think, Tayt, think.

I've been in worse spots before. None immediately spring to mind, but I'm sure I have at some point. I crabwalk toward the rear of the apartment, then realize I've left all the locks on the door undone. At least I closed the door. But should I change direction and try to slide the deadbolts closed before the officer gets to the door? If I don't, I'm a sitting duck. Unless the officer is pretty sure there is someone in here and that person is armed and dangerous, I don't think he or she will break down a locked door to get in. Right?

My brain scrambles madly to think of what C.J. would do in this situation, but between my racing heartbeat and loud breathing, I can't think clearly.

Switching direction mid-crabwalk, I nearly tumble over. The blue strobe lights are so bright in the otherwise dark room that I feel like I'm at a rave.

There are footsteps on the stairs.

Groping wildly, I ease one of the locks into place. Or try to. It's stuck and won't budge.

The footsteps are getting louder. I try the second deadbolt. This one screeches as the two pieces of the metal meet. I throw the third lock, no longer caring about the noise, and scoot back away from the door. The footsteps stop just outside the door.

Chapter Ten

A knock sounds, loud and quick. I'm halfway to the kitchen and about to see what lies outside the bedroom window. If the drop isn't too far, or if there is a porch or other low roof below, I might have a chance.

Another knock, insistent.

I poke my head out the back window. There are thirty empty feet between me and a gravel parking area below.

Screw that.

Even if I got the sheets knotted and secured before letting myself out, there is likely a second officer and/or K-9 unit in the car to watch my descent. Or are they both stationed outside Mark's front door? I retrace my steps to the door, not bothering to crouch anymore. They know someone is in here, why bother pretending I'm part of the *Mission Impossible* team?

Heart still hammering in my ribcage, I walk directly to the door, unlock the deadbolts, and stand, ready to face my punishment. But the figure at the door is young and has longish hair and smells faintly like manure.

"You're not a cop," I say stupidly.

"Nah, man. I'm wondering who called them. The old lady?" He nods his head sideways toward the door of apartment three.

"I'm Derrick, by the way. Who are you?"

I answer without thinking, "Lindsay. Nice to meet you. I'm just stopped over at Mark's to, um, pick something up."

Derrick nods and looks down the stairs toward the blue orbs whirling in the dark street.

"You know what's happening?" he asks.

I shake my head. My heart rate is now semi-normal and I feel like jumping up and down and kissing Derrick on the cheek for not being a police officer. I restrain myself.

"No idea."

"Huh. Well, I'm guessing they're not coming this way. Still, might want to hide your stash, if you know what I mean."

"Right. Good idea."

"G'night."

I watch Derrick tromp back down the stairs. Then I retreat into the dark apartment and lean against the closed door.

***

The next evening, I settle into a club chair near the coffeehouse window, balancing a plate with a pastry and a steaming mug of coffee. Ezra flops into the chair nearest me, his long legs splayed in front of him. He's already eaten half of his first donut and crumbs tumble down his beard and shirt.

I laugh, nodding toward his front. "Going to get any of that in your mouth?"

He smiles back, picks some of the crumbs off his chest and pops them into his mouth, then takes a long sip of tea. He's the only man I know who prefers tea to coffee.

"So what did you think of the movie?" he asks.

I move my plate to a little round table near us and take a sip of coffee. The heat of the mug feels good on my cold fingers.

"It wasn't bad. Could have had a little more storyline and a little less gore, but I've seen worse. Did you like it?"

Ezra nods, then shakes his head. "Could have had a little less storyline and a little more gore. Other than that, not bad. But not the worst I've seen, you're right."

We sip and chew in silence for several minutes. It's a comfortable silence, though, like that between two people who have known each other for a long, long time and don't feel the need to constantly make small talk. Old-time jazz plays on the speakers overhead.

Ezra stares out the window, lost in thought, and I absorb the décor of the coffee shop. It features new artwork monthly. I haven't been in for a while, so it's all new to me. This month's artist appears to be a minimalist, painting with only white, a brown so dark it's nearly black, and a pale yellow. The effect is…odd.

Ezra has finished his donuts and is reading headlines out of yesterday's newspaper. I continue nibbling my pastry, some flaky thing filled with almond crème, and listen as he reads the Dear Paula column.

"Huh. Listen to this one. Wounded in Kentucky wrote last week, 'Dear Paula, my husband of seven years has been cheating on me. I just found out after arriving home from a tour of duty in Afghanistan. I do not want to seek counseling but would love to hear of any of your readers' ideas for revenge, particularly humiliating ones.'"

I laugh. "At least she's honest. What did Paula have to say to that?" I ask, taking another bite of the pastry. Gooey, warm filling hits the roof of my mouth and lingers.

He is quiet for a few minutes, then says, "She didn't suggest the woman seek revenge."

I snort at this. "Of course not. Read it, please."

"She says, 'Dear Wounded: Revenge is an ugly word and won't undo what your husband has done. You're hurt and need time to heal. Please consider counseling and, if necessary, separation from your husband to process your feelings.'"

"Oh, please. I've got some ideas I'd be happy to share with Wounded," I say.

"You're not the only one. Dear Paula opened the question up to her readers in this week's column. Read some of these." Ezra hands me the paper.

I put my plate on the table and take the paper, Ezra's calloused fingers bumping mine. Five different writers have tackled the problem, suggesting everything from reconciliation to posting the most unflattering pictures possible on every social network available with the word "ADULTERER" attached to each. I laugh out loud at that one.

"Is that the 'adulterer' one?" Ezra asks.

I nod, handing the paper back.

"What do you think, Ez? You're practically a priest now. Should Wounded forgive her husband and welcome him home with open arms?" I ask sarcastically. I don't know why I feel the desire to needle him. Maybe I haven't quite gotten past what he's said about my dad. Ezra's take on my parents' relationship still makes me feel hot and itchy when I think about it, which I try to avoid doing.

Ezra grimaces at me, shifts in his seat.

"Forgiveness isn't about making yourself into a doormat. If the guy is sorry and if the woman wants to work it out, then they probably have a chance. But it sounds like she doesn't. So, chances are they won't."

"But what counsel would you give? I mean, as a priest. I'm curious what goes on in your mind."

"I guess we haven't gotten that far in my Confessional 101 class yet," Ezra says, smiling.

Not for the first time, I wonder what Ezra would think of my Sunflower Specials. I've imagined telling him many times. Once, after too much champagne at a New Year's Eve party, I'd nearly blurted it all out, while the people around us hugged and kissed and brokenly sang *Auld Lang Syne.* Something in me—some bit of common sense I'd retained—had held me back. I was so grateful the next day. But sometimes even now, I wish I could tell him. That he'd tell me he understood what I was doing and why. I don't expect him to approve of it—that would be pushing it too far. But just to see and accept it, I guess.

I prop my ankles on his chair. "But what about in general?" I ask. "What do you think about retaliation or the punishment of crimes outside the law? I don't mean a spouse cheating, but something more...I don't know, rogue?"

Ezra raises his eyebrows. "Are we still talking about hypotheticals here, or is there something you want to tell me?"

"Hypothetically, of course," I say, while a little voice sing-songs about Sunflower Specials in my brain.

"Let's just say, for instance, that you had a sister," I continue. "Or me. Let's say me. Someone comes after me and beats me up or abducts and kills me. If you had the chance to get even with that person afterward and no one would find out about it, would you?"

"Define getting even."

"You know. Beat them to death, drive them off a cliff, drown them."

"You've spent some time thinking about this," he says. He's still smiling but his eyes look different, distant.

I sip some coffee and lean my head back in the chair.

"Personally, as a man and your friend, of course, I would want to do all that and worse. But I'm not just a man, I'm also someone who has been forgiven for things I've done—some of them pretty bad."

"Oh, come on," I say teasingly. "You, doing bad things?"

He shakes his head. "I did plenty when I was messed up and high or wanting to get high. Ugly stuff." His face wears a shadow suddenly and his eyes have lost the crinkles around the edges. "Ugly stuff," he says again, his voice a whisper.

Regret pools in my belly and I tilt my head, looking at the man I know as well as the outline of my own face. We'd grown apart during that time in his life. I was caught up in problems with my family and escapist dreams of making it as a successful actor. We'd still been young when Ezra had fallen in with the wrong crowd while his parents' marriage (which had been dysfunctional at best, abusive at worst) disintegrated. He'd moved in with my family for a while, my mother convincing my dad that it was the right thing to do. But not long after that, Ezra had gotten in serious trouble. He'd been sent to a juvenile delinquent center in the southern part of the state.

"Sorry," I say now. "Sometimes I forget that whole period of your life."

He shrugs. "I try to forget it too, as much as I can."

"Well, let me ask you one thing more about this, and then I promise I'll stop. Let's say that a person has gone through the legal system, but for whatever reason—bad evidence, an unsympathetic jury, a crooked judge—that person never saw their perpetrator punished. Would it be wrong for them to exact some form of punishment? A punishment that would have been doled out by our judicial system in a perfect world?"

"But the world isn't perfect, Tayt. And even if this person got the revenge they felt that they deserved, it wouldn't undo what had been done to them. And to tell you the truth, it would probably make their life harder, not better."

I raise my eyebrows but say nothing.

"Statistics show that people who win the lottery end up unhappy in the long-term, more than those people who don't. Did you know that?"

"No."

"Because the things that we think are going to heal us and make us feel better—the dreams of being rich and success-ful, the desire to prove to the world that we're somebody with power, even the desire to get even like you're talking about—those things, in the end, don't make us happy. They're just empty promises."

I sigh through my nose and put my feet back on the floor. "I don't know. It seems to me like winning the lottery would take care of a lot of my problems. How could getting rid of all my debt be a negative?"

"Maybe there's some lesson that you're supposed to learn through the process."

I snort, fold up the paper. "The lesson I want to learn is how to balance my checkbook at the end of the month and find out that there is lots of leftover money I don't know what to do with."

"Well, if you do win the lottery, throw a little of it my way, huh?" Ezra says. "I'm pretty sure that the article said sharing the wealth made the lottery-winners much happier."

I laugh and then my phone rings. I answer without checking

the number.

"This is Tayt."

"Tayt? It's Phil. Phil Hunley. We spoke the other day."

"Oh, hey, Phil, how's it going?"

The voice on the other end of the phone is shaking a little. Nerves?

Ezra raises his eyebrows at me and points to his watch. He has some monk ritual at four o'clock in the morning.

I motion with my free hand that I'm ready and he puts our dishes into the bin by the coffee counter. We zip our coats simultaneously, me pressing the cell phone between shoulder and chin.

"So, listen, that event I was talking about, it's coming right up," Phil says. "Are you still going to be able to make it?"

"Oh, um, yeah, sure. What was it again?" I rack my brain trying to remember if he'd ever spelled out what he'd needed security help with. Concert? Poker tournament?

"I don't think we ever discussed the details," Phil says. "It's, um, a party," he adds. "At my parents' house."

"Okay. How many people attending?"

"How many…" his voice fades out. "How many people?"

"Yeah, I need to know the number of people to know if I need to hire some extra hands. Generally, if the crowd is about twentyish or under, I'm okay on my own. If it's much more than that, though, I like to hire a couple of local guys to help out. How many do you think will be attending?"

Silence.

"Hello? Are you there?" I ask.

Ezra motions toward the door and mimics walking. I nod and fall in step behind him, then follow him onto the sidewalk, winding a scarf around my neck at the same time.

"Well, ah, see, this isn't a big party."

"Okay. So you just need me, is that what you're saying?"

"Yes. Sort of."

I sigh. It's too late in the day to have much left in the patience reservoir.

"Phil, I feel like we're having two different conversations here. You want to hire me to handle security at this party, correct?"

Pause.

"Well, no, not exactly."

"So, what exactly is it that you want me to do?" I'm over-enunciating my words and Ezra starts laughing under his breath.

"Uh, well, be my date," Phil says.

"Be your date?" I parrot back stupidly.

Ezra turns around and wiggles an eyebrow up and down. His chuckle turns into a big, Cheshire-cat grin. I smack him on the arm and keep walking.

"Right. At the party. I need a date and figured—"

"You want to hire me to be your date. Like a call girl?"

"No, no. Not like that. It's complicated. I can't ask...that is...I can't—" Phil lets out a whoosh of frustrated breath. "My parents expect me to have a date. So, I'd like to hire you to do it. It's not anything sexual if that's what you're worried about."

My brain is struggling to keep up with this odd conversation.

"Okay," I say slowly. "You know there are escort services that would probably be a better fit for this type of thing."

"No, please." Phil sighs. "This is hard enough as it is. At least I know you."

There's a beat of silence, then he says, "Look, I know this is weird, but my fiancée...died. And I haven't been able to date since then. My parents, well, they don't understand how hard it is for me to get back out there. They've been pushing me to date again, but I just can't. Anyway, this party is for their fortieth anniversary. It's very posh and all their richy-rich friends will be there. My job as their one and only son is to show up with an attractive female and be attentive and engaging and make all their friends *ooh* and *ahh* over what a great job they did as parents." Phil gives a strangled-sounding chuckle.

Part of me still feels weirded out to be hired as a date. Another part of me is flattered that he considers me an "attractive female." Then I realize he hasn't seen me since high school.

"So, will you still do it?" he asks.

I chew the inside of my cheek. Ezra nudges me with his shoulder and gives me a questioning look. I ignore him.

"Sure," I tell Phil.

He sighs loudly on the other end of the phone. "Great. Thank you."

"So, when is this shindig?" I ask. "And what am I supposed to wear?"

Chapter Eleven

The next morning, I'm at the gym and working out hard—well, harder than I have in a long time. Compared to workouts I was doing before my injury, this is fluff. I block that out. Now, not only am I trying to get my strength back, but also my figure. Phil is going to be billed for the party dress, but I want to get something I might actually wear again. The only guidelines he gave me were that it had to be formal and something in an eye-catching color.

Ezra had nearly doubled over with laughter when I'd explained the full phone conversation last night.

"I don't see what's so funny," I'd finally said after he'd laughed himself nearly to tears. "Is having me as a date so hilarious?"

"No," Ezra had wheezed, wiping tears from the corners of his eyes. "You just get yourself into the strangest situations."

I'd snorted. Was it my fault that people asked for help with unusual problems? I'd left him on the curb in front of the shrine's truck, still chuckling. Then I'd spent the rest of the night thinking about how awkward this party was going to be. Shouldn't Phil and I meet first, make sure we have our story straight? It's going to look a little weird if he says we met one way and I'm telling everyone we met another.

I make a mental note to call and ask him about this at the

same time the heavy bag swings back in my direction. I hit it with a right jab and then a sharp left hook. Pain radiates from my shoulder and into the other side of my body.

Gritting my teeth, I hit the bag again and again. Pain or not, it feels good to be back at the gym, where people don't ask questions—fussing and fretting over *how are you feeling? are you overexerting?*—and just let me get on with my workout.

After I finish and stretch, I head to the showers. The stalls are empty and I choose the one farthest back, stripping out of my sweaty clothes in the privacy area and stepping into the stall. A cloud of hot water vapor engulfs me and I turn and let the spray wash over my head and down my back. My fingers automatically go to the spot, tracing the area of red, puckered skin.

At first, it bothered me to look at it. It was so angry and ugly. Raw, red skin twisted. Now though, I'm beginning to see it as a sign of bravery, a badge of honor. Maybe I'll get a tattoo over it someday like women who lose a breast to cancer.

The door to the locker room opens and closes and I hear footsteps. I wait to hear another shower turn on but there's no sound. Maybe someone lost track of the time and is making do with a sponge bath. But no water runs and there is no sound of a locker opening and closing. I debate peeking my head out but the water feels good and the air outside the stall will be cold. I shrug, lather my hair and rinse, soaping up while the conditioner (which promises to protect my delicate ends from splitting) does its thing. I'm about to rinse it out and shave my legs when the door opens again. I don't hear it close.

It's while I'm drying off and dressing, hair pulled into a turban, that I see something poking out of my gym bag. It's white and square. What is it? I dry my hands on the towel on my head before walking over and pulling it out. A single piece of white copier paper, folded in four. I open it and see two words. They are centered on the paper.

"I'm watching."

The letters are boxy, cut from a newspaper. There's no name, no other marks on the paper. I fold the paper back up carefully and put it into the side pocket of my bag. Too much coffee, I tell myself. That's why my fingers are shaking.

I comb my hair out and dry it halfheartedly, my arms too tired to finish the job. Then I dress and carry my bag to the hallway. I retrace my steps to the check-in desk. Bundling into outerwear, I wave to the guy behind the high desk.

"Hey, did you notice anyone going to the women's locker room about ten minutes ago?" I ask.

The guy (whose name I can't remember) is big and beefy but with surprisingly small, elegant-looking hands. He shakes his head, a bandana covering a ring of wavy, dark hair.

"Nah, sorry, I didn't. Any problems?"

"No, no problem. I just thought I heard someone come in, that's all. Have a good day," I say and head for the door.

***

I debate with myself on my drive to the office. Should I leave the note with the police or just ignore it? I could call C.J. and sic him on it. But then he'll only ask me more questions, get more protective. I can barely stand all the smothering as it is. Forget it. It's probably a practical joke. Or maybe the note was meant for someone else.

At the office, I distract myself by Googling West Fresh Institute, the place Mark had written in his notebook. The air is still chilly in the big room and I pull on an extra bomber jacket that I keep behind the door. The fabric is heavy and cold at first, but the silk lining warms quickly. I tap my Doc Martins impatiently, waiting for the page to load. My stomach growls but I ignore it.

Finally, the page finishes loading. West Fresh Institute is a vegan, raw food culinary school. It's a residential program, offering everything from classes for weekend cooks to serious students looking for a professional culinary arts degree. The food looks like sculptures and is incredibly colorful compared to the pathetic sandwiches I usually eat. I mentally pat myself on the back for a couple of visits to the Juice Bar recently. But that doesn't stop me from reaching into the top desk drawer as I read about the class offerings of the school, what a typical semester looks like, and pulling out a bag of peanut butter-filled pretzels. Just a few. To tide me over until lunch.

Clicking back to the home page, I position my pretzel to the side of the computer. (I hate crumbs lodged in the keys.) I find the culinary school's phone number and do some quick math in my head. It's just past ten here, which would make it, what, seven there?

It's pretty early, but I dial anyway. There are three sharp rings and then a woman's recorded voice invites me to explore the health-sustaining offerings of West Fresh Institute by selecting one of the following numbered menu options. I press the number for admissions and am surprised when another woman's voice answers—this time a real, live person.

My brain swirls with ideas. I hadn't expected anyone to answer. What do I do? Tell a lie? The truth? What will get me the information I'm looking for?

I clear my throat. "Hello, I'm hoping you can put me in touch with my brother, Mark. Mark Chester. He's just started at the school."

There's a pause and I wait for the woman to tell me that she can't give out that type of personal information or to ask my name. I search my brain wildly for something appropriate. Sue? Melissa? Cindy? Something that won't stand out too much in her memory.

"I'm sorry, ma'am." I wait for her to tell me the next bit—"We don't give out that kind of information"—but instead she says, "Mark is in class right now. Our students start their day early. Class has been running for a half-hour now. I'd be happy to take a message for you and give it to him if you'd like."

"Oh, um, no, that's okay. I'll just try him back later."

"Sure, no problem. Have a health-filled day."

"Thanks, you too," I say and hang up.

I can't resist pumping a fist in the air briefly. The prodigal son (or boyfriend, rather) has been found. I call Garrison's Gym and get Sandra on the phone.

"Good news," I say. "I found Mark."

She squeals on the other end, so loudly that I pull the phone away from my ear to protect my eardrum.

"That's wonderful news. Good job!"

"Thanks. It seems that he's out west, in Arizona. I wasn't sure how you wanted me to proceed from here, so I thought I would give you a call."

"Arizona? Hold on a second." There is a loud clunk and I hear Sandra greeting someone in the room, then there are a few seconds of dead air, a click, and she's back on the line.

"Sorry, I just walked in and wanted to go into the office for more privacy. What is he doing in Arizona?"

"He's at a vegan, raw foods culinary institute. It's called West

Fresh Institute. I'm not sure how long he's planning to stay, though. He could be registered for just a short-term class or he could be there for the duration of the program—that runs two years."

Sandra makes a disgruntled sound.

"But his apartment hasn't been cleaned out," I say, hoping she won't ask how I know this. I rush on, "I called his landlord, but he hasn't called me back yet. I'll try him again today, see what he knows. I just thought you'd want an update and to know that he's okay."

"Yes, thanks so much. I appreciate it." Sandra's voice fades away and for a second I think I've lost her. When she speaks again, her voice is clear, though. "The strange thing is"—she exhales sharply—"we talked about doing this together, him and me. I find it hard to believe he'd just take off without me. You're sure he's registered?"

"I just got off the phone with someone in admissions."

There are a few seconds of silence and I picture Sandra twirling a lock of blonde hair around her finger. I have no idea if this is actually one of her habits, but she seems like someone who would be a hair-twister.

"Well," she says at last, "I think you'll need to book a flight out there."

"A flight?" I repeat dumbly. Half of me is jumping up and down (free vacation!) and the other half is ready to screech in frustration. I have other cases I'm working on, however slowly, and I can't just jet off across the country.

"I'll pay your travel expenses, of course, and I'll give you double the fee in our contract if you bring him back with you."

Well, then.

"Sure," I say. "That works for me."

Chapter Twelve

As I'm driving home, I replay the phone call with Mark's landlord in my mind. No, he didn't know that his renter was out of town. No, he wasn't concerned. And no, (obviously) he had no idea when Mark was expected back. Not super helpful. In addition to worrying about my trip and all the loose ends I want to have tied up before leaving, I have Phil's party coming up and this stupid note to deal with. Or not deal with. I glance toward my gym bag reflexively.

Another incoming call interrupts my thoughts. I glance at the screen and nearly groan. My mother. I wedge my Bluetooth into my ear and answer.

"Hi, Mama," I say, trying to sound chipper instead of stressed and irritated.

"Tatum Rose, it is so good to hear your voice. I hope you've been spending a lot of time resting." My mother's voice is saccharine sweet. "I have another stack of magazines for you."

Mama keeps giving me home decorating and fashion magazines as though she's trying to tell me something.

"Remember what the doctor said: You'll never heal properly if you take on too much, too soon."

I tune out for a few minutes. Watch the lines in the road.

Think about the pint of Ben & Jerry's sitting in the freezer.

"…which is why I'm calling," she says after several seconds of silence on my end. "She'll be arriving tonight," she continues, "and I hoped you might be able to pick her up at the airport. It's such a short trip. I told her there was no reason to rent a car. You don't mind collecting her, do you, darling?"

Conundrum: Do I admit that I wasn't listening and have no idea who I'm supposed to collect at the airport or just agree and find out when I get there?

"Um, sure. Yes, I can do that."

"Oh, that's wonderful. Thank you, Tatum."

"No problem." I feel instantly guilty that I don't call the woman more often. I'm the only one of her children who lives close enough to visit and I don't even call her once a week. What kind of daughter am I?

"I know that you and Sophie have your differences, but it's so good to see you making an effort to be a good sister." My mother's southern drawl is thicker than usual. It happens when she's emotional.

But wait. What does Sophie have to do with it?

Oh, no. I clap a hand on my forehead and then replace it onto the wheel before the car veers into a ditch. *No, no, no, no.* I did not just agree to collect Sophie from the airport, did I?

"You're sure it won't take too much out of you?"

I mumble something that must sound like the answer Mama wants because she continues. "She'll be arriving on the seven o'clock flight from Philadelphia. You might want to call the airport just before you leave to make sure everything's on schedule. Hopefully, that storm will hold off until she's home safe and sound."

Storm?

I assure my mother that I will call the airport before I leave and ask if she'd like to come along for the ride. She doesn't drive but generally loves to be invited anywhere.

"Not this time, baby. I'll have dinner for y'all in the oven and the dogs will be resting. It might be stressful for them if plans change suddenly. And you know how Grover is, bless his little heart."

I do, in fact, know how my mother's neurotic dogs are—particularly Grover, who pees on the floor if his schedule is altered. Or his kibble is varied. Or the water bowl has hair in it.

I sigh, close my eyes for a second.

"Okay," I say weakly. "I'll see you tonight, then."

"Sounds wonderful. Thanks again, Tatum."

I want to say, "Oh, no problem, and thank you for calling and dropping this steaming pile of dog doo in my lap at the last minute."

"Sure," I say instead. "Anytime, Mama."

***

It's as I'm driving to the airport that night (prayers for the giant storm of the century still unanswered, though I'm checking the sky for a last-minute miracle) that my heart skips a beat. Out of the nothingness of the empty road comes a genius idea about how to deal with Emerson Prescott. At least, I think it's genius. Driving has this effect on me, a way of unwinding my mind and letting all its background work come to the surface as the miles speed past.

I grin and mentally pat myself on the back. With a plan for Prescott, I can now focus on my trip. I haven't been to Arizona before. What better time to go than during a never-ending frozen stretch in Vermont? I wonder if I can weave this impromptu trip into the conversation with Sophie. Our exchanges always leave me feeling like an uneducated hick with hay pieces stuck in my hair while Sophie, polished and perfect, looks down her expensively powdered nose at me.

The night is clear and cold, stars pressed into the dark sky above like pieces of chunky glitter. I leave the parking garage, hustling to get into the warmth of the airport. Cold air whips across the open corridor that separates the two buildings. A lone plane circles overhead, ready to land. The sound is deafening. The automatic doors open and close, and the sound of the aircraft is drowned out when I enter the building.

Instantly, my nose is assaulted by heavily fragranced candles. To the right is a small gift shop where the horrible things reside. The shop is overflowing with Vermont-themed gifts: Stuffed moose, cows, and maple-flavored everything. I walk upstairs toward the incoming gates, checking a monitor on my way.

The flight from Philadelphia is on time. *Crap.*

The airport is small—so tiny, in fact, that there are waiting areas outside of each of the handful of gates. I find a molded plastic chair outside Sophie's gate and sit. My legs feel jittery and my arms won't be still, though, so I pace the area instead. A few families are waiting, plus a guy in his thirties with a bouquet. An older couple bends over a phone, looking at pictures. Their faces are lined, free hands clasped.

I swallow and realize my throat's dry. A trip to the water fountain around the corner helps. I use the bathroom while I'm in the area, taking my time washing my hands. Checking my reflection in the mirror, seeing the same brown eyes and straight, brown hair I've had since childhood. (Well, other than the time I tried a perm. Can you say "poodle?") I apply a coat of lip gloss, smooth my hands through my hair, and pinch my cheeks, hoping it will disguise my nose that's still red from the cold. I hear an overhead announcement. Sucking in my gut, I head back to the gate.

Sophie arrives minutes later in a cloud of expensive perfume. She's wearing a perfectly cut suit (who wears a suit when not at work?) and a new, shorter hairstyle, very swingy and very blonde. Her eyes are as blue as ever and she's lost weight. If she loses more, she may become transparent.

I feel like a cow lumbering toward her, my boots clomping and the jeans I squeezed into constricting around my waist like a noose.

"Oh, Tatum, it's you." Her brow wrinkles, making two perfect lines above her eyes. Her mouth pulls down into a little disgruntled bow. She looks so much like our mother. Only a younger and more stunning version.

"Mama asked if I could give you a ride home." Oddly, we both refer to Mama's cottage—which neither of us has ever lived in—as home.

"Well, thank you. That's…nice of you," Sophie says.

We hesitate for a second and then I pull her into an awkward hug. It's like trying to hug an ironing board. I let go and she sniffs, smiles, and strides toward the staircase which leads to the baggage claim area. "I suppose it works out well for you, too. Probably don't get to Burlington very often?"

I shake my head. "Nope, us country bumpkins don't make it off the farm too often. Not like you, big sis." I match my walk to my hick accent, swaggering as though I just came off the back of a horse, and steal a look in her direction.

She exhales sharply. "Please, stop. You are embarrassing me."

"Aw, gee, didn't mean to embarrass you, ma'am," I say, exaggerating my swagger even more. "We hicks from the sticks don't know much about city livin', that's for sure."

Sophie ignores me and stalks ahead, walking surprisingly fast on very skinny, extremely high heels. I stop swaggering and walk several paces behind, like a kid dragging her feet after her mother tells her to hurry up. What is it about Sophie and Mama that brings out my inner brat?

A small crowd grows near one of the two baggage carousels. People murmur together in small groups. You can tell who lives here—they're the ones dressed in layers of warm clothing. The rest of the people have on thin jackets and light windbreakers. Sophie shivers every time the nearby automatic doors open, bringing in a blast of arctic air.

"I've got an extra coat in the car," I say, walking up to her. My head is just a bit over shoulder level, and I wonder if my attitude has something to do with the fact that I literally feel five years old near my sister. There is no justice in genetics, that's for sure.

"Thanks," she says, "but I have some warmer things in my suitcase."

At that moment, there's a loud bleat from the baggage claim carousel and a red strobe light starts spinning. Everyone takes an unconscious step or two forward, as though willing their luggage to come out first.

We wait several minutes and then a perfectly glossy, white suitcase spills out onto the belt. Sophie takes a deep breath before moving forward to collect it—preparing for the weight, most likely. I reach for it at the same time and together with our hands on the thick handle, we wrestle it to the ground.

"What did you pack in here, bricks?" I ask.

"I brought some extra clothes; I knew it would be cold. And a few gifts for Mama."

"Gifts like rocks?"

Sophie ignores me and yanks the handle out of the case, enabling it to glide along smoothly over the polished floor.

"Let's just go, okay?" she says and heads toward the door.

***

By the time we arrive at our mother's cottage, my rusted, old Toyota has finally heated up fully. Sophie is still shivering, despite the thick coat she'd pulled from her luggage and the extra one I keep under the seat that she'd spread over her bare legs.

A light snow falls. The cottage, with its warm light blazing in the windows and the snowflakes soundlessly dancing down, looks like a Christmas card scene. The spell is broken by Grover and Ashford, Mama's two annoying dogs, bounding from the cottage. There's plenty of jumping, dashing, slipping, and sliding as they rush to the car and determine if the occupants are friend or foe. Never mind that I've had this car for eight years and that Sophie and I held the dogs when they were puppies and were cuter and less stupid.

"Grover and Ashford! Is that the polite way to greet our guests?" my mother sings out from the top step.

The house is cream-colored, looking more like an advertisement in a glossy home decorating magazine than a real, lived-in home. A small red barn stands nearby, where one could park a car if one could drive (my mother doesn't) and another building, a miniature version of the cottage, stands beyond that. My mother calls it her retreat. Since she lives alone, I'm not sure what she's retreating from. I suspect it's her annoying dogs.

Speaking of annoying, the second I crack the door of my car—which opens with a loud squeal—Grover sticks half of his body into the space and immediately jams his nose into my crotch. This is reason number seventy-nine why I do not have a dog. Sophie smartly stays motionless and leaves her door unopened until Mama calls off the dogs. They retreat, bouncing and barking, into the house.

"Sorry about that, darlings. You know how much they love you," Mama says, picking her way across the snowy driveway to the passenger's side of the car.

"If they loved us any more, we'd be wearing them," I say. I hear a thin tinkle of laughter from Sophie's side of the car. On this one, ridiculously small matter, Sophie and I agree.

Mama puts her hands on her hips.

"Now, Tatum, you know they do. Oh, Sophie!" my mother gasps. "Don't you look stunning?" She opens my sister's door. "I love your new haircut."

My lips immediately form a smart-aleck comment, but I bite my tongue, hard, and pull my sister's jumbo-sized luggage from the back seat. Or try to. When she sees me struggling, my sister takes pity on me and helps extract it. It took a while to wedge it into place. For a few scary seconds I think it's not coming back out. Finally, though, with much tugging and some cursing on my part, it emerges.

Sophie drifts off, answering Mama's question that I couldn't hear over my ragged panting. I roll the suitcase toward the house, my sister and mother ahead of me. Mama's soft Southern accent has that trilling sound it gets when she is excited. Of course, she's excited. Her golden child is safely home.

Stop it. For pity's sake, you're not five years old anymore.

My foot catches on a rock near the path to the door and I nearly fall.

"Careful, Tatum," Sophie says.

What's this? I pause, my hand sweating on the handle. Is my sister showing actual loving concern for me?

She glances back over her shoulder. "There are breakables in there."

Chapter Thirteen

I fake an incoming phone call during dinner. Anything to get out of the overly warm, overly perfumed dining room. Grover trots on my heels but as soon as we're out of my mother's sight, I nudge him away with my knee. He looks at me in wonderment, as though no one has ever refused his presence before. I make a face at him. He wags his tail and comes closer, pressing his hairy, shedding side against my legs. Finally, I lock myself into the bathroom.

Once there, I decide to make good use of the time and call Reba. There is no answer on her cell phone, so I try the barn.

"Yeah," a gruff man's voice says.

I hang up. Chew a hangnail. Then I call again.

Same greeting, this time even more impatient-sounding.

"So sorry, I must have gotten disconnected. I'm trying to reach Reba. Is she there?"

"Who wants to know?"

None of your business.

I smile. I read somewhere that doing so puts the person on the other end of the phone in a better frame of mind. The way this guy sounds, I may need to grin like a clown.

"This is her gynecologist's office."

"It's almost nine at night," the man says.

"Yes, well, in these instances we prefer to pass along the information right away. If you could just get Reba—"

"Hold your horses," he grunts.

There's a loud clunk and I hear a machine whirring and a couple of cows mooing in the background. Several long minutes later, Reba answers.

"I have an idea that I think will work. Do you want to meet in the morning and talk about it?"

"What?" Reba's voice sounds far away. "I can't hear you. Who is this?"

"It's—" I nearly say "Tayt" and catch myself at the last second. "It's me. Sunflower Specials."

There's a loud click on her end of the phone and for a minute I think she's hung up on me. But when Reba comes back on the line her voice is clearer.

"Who is this?"

"Sunflower Specials."

"Oh. Good. Do you have a plan?" Her voice is quieter.

"Yes. I thought you might want to meet tomorrow morning to go over it. And I'll need payment—half, at least—up front."

This is the part where I hold my breath. I hate asking for money for doing Sunflower Specials. It seems wrong somehow, that I'm tainting something good. But Visa and the mortgage company are unrelenting taskmasters.

"Yeah, all right. I can meet you at the Rail Trail again. I'm done milking about eleven. Can you meet me around then?"

I tell her yes and we say our goodbyes.

***

Sophie and my mother are lingering over cups of coffee, and I pour myself a mug, adding cream and sugar.

"The easiest way to get rid of those extra pounds," Sophie says, pointing at the sugar bowl. "Cut down on your carbs."

I swallow a retort and look at the clock. Are the batteries dead? How can the minute hand have only moved *that* much in the time I was gone?

"Thanks, Sophie, but we can't all subsist on water and air alone." I stir my coffee too briskly and a little of it slops over the side of the cup. "Yes, I've put on a few pounds. So, shoot me. Oh, that's right, someone already did!" I laugh.

My mother frowns, though. "Sophie is only trying to offer some friendly advice," she says. Her long fingers are pale against the dark cup.

I snort in response.

"When you get shot for the first time, Sophie, let me know how many classes you're taking at the gym, okay?" I set my mug down too hard and Grover bounces close to the table for a look. "Give me a break," I say under my breath.

Sophie nods. "Fine, Tatum, I was just trying to be helpful. As usual, you are determined to twist everything I say into criticism."

"Imagine that."

My mother shoots me a dark look and I take a sip of coffee as a preventative measure.

"So, tell us where the idea for this impromptu trip came from," says my mother, changing the subject and leaning toward Sophie.

My sister stares out the dark window. She seems to shrink in front of my eyes. Instead of looking glamorous and perfect, Sophie looks suddenly unstarched, her face gray in the light, her eyes smudged with bruise-like shadows.

"I've left Elliot," she says finally.

"Oh, baby doll," Mama says. She draws back in her chair shaking her head, one hand at her throat. Mama's unconscious way of showing shock.

A few long, quiet seconds pass.

"What happened?" Mama asks finally. She removes the hand from her slender neck and puts it over my sister's hand. Sophie is motionless, her eyes glassy as she continues to look through the window.

"The whole thing that happened with…with Dad. It's been weighing on me. I've been thinking a lot about life and what matters and what doesn't."

"Having your father accused of murder can do that to a person," I say. "Can you pass the almonds?"

My mother frowns more deeply at me. Sophie turns, her eyes boring into mine. I squirm in my seat.

"What?" I say, my voice innocent. "I just don't see how Dad's situation has anything to do with your marriage. I mean, I thought you liked Elliot. Plus, third time's the charm and all that—"

"What is wrong with you?" she interrupts. "Are you so intimidated by my success that it prevents you from having a civil conversation? You are so immature, Tatum. I wish you'd never…" Her voice drifts off.

Never what? Been invited to dinner? Been born? I (not for the first time) picture Sophie as an only child. She would have loved every minute of it.

I stand up, my chair soundless on the tile floor.

"I'm fairly sure that's my cue. I have a busy day tomorrow," I say.

My mother leaps from her chair and comes around the table. I half expect her to shove me back into my seat, but she pauses just before she gets to me and puts her hand on my arm.

"Please stay, Tatum. Your sister needs you."

Sophie has never needed anyone, not in her whole life, except maybe an audience. Just applause and admiration. I don't say this, though, figuring I've opened my fat mouth too much as it is.

"I've got to go, Mama. Thanks for dinner." I reach for my mother, plant a kiss on her cheek. She smells like Coco Chanel and flour. I stay where I am just a second longer than necessary, breathing.

My mother has never been a good hugger. She sort of stands there and does nothing, as though she's enduring a hug more than enjoying it. My father, though, used to give great hugs: big and boisterous and tight. But that was a long time ago.

"Sophie," I let go of my mother and turn to my sister. She's staring again in that glassy-eyed way. "I'm sorry about Elliot." I half hunch over, wrap my arm around her shoulders, and squeeze quickly before pulling away.

"Maybe you can make it work. He's a..." I stumble because the words "tedious" and "dull" are the first that come to mind. "He's a nice guy."

She nods, turns her gaze to the table, and watches a tea light flickering.

The dogs walk me to the door. Well, actually, they sandwich me between them and walk in the direction of the door. I stuff my arms into thick coat sleeves, pull on a hat and a pair of ratty woolen gloves, and let myself out of the house, pushing them back in with my knee before closing the door behind me.

Stupid. Stupid. Stupid.

Sophie had a point, much as it pains me to admit it. What *is* wrong with me? Why can't I ever keep my mouth shut?

Because you really are jealous, a little voice says. *Because Sophie is a success and rich and beautiful, and you are none of those.*

Well. There is that.

***

I meet Reba at twenty past eleven the next morning. Her nose is red with cold, and her cheeks are pink. Her hair is short and curly, and it stands out around the edge of a warm-looking but ugly hat like party ribbons.

I clasp her hand in mine when we meet. Hers are calloused and rough, making mine feel surprisingly ladylike in her firm grasp.

The wind blows down the corridor created by the trees bordering the bike path and I shiver.

"Let's walk," I say.

Reba nods and falls into step with me. I shove my hands into my pockets and try to get the blood circulating in my fingers again by rubbing them together in little circles.

"Here's what I've been thinking…" I say, and outline a plan.

Ten minutes later, we stop in the path, Reba looking at me like I've just suggested a cure for cancer and she's won the lottery all at once.

"There's no guarantee it will work, though," I say. "You know that, right?"

Nod.

Reba picks a well-worn leather wallet from her jeans and empties the billfold, handing me a wad of cash. I flip through

it quickly, counting under my breath, then nod and thank her.
"So, here's what I'll need…"

Chapter Fourteen

The next day dawns with gun-metal gray skies. My flight is scheduled to leave Burlington at four-thirty. The storm we'd thought had blown past us has returned. Thick, wet snow has been coming down for the past few hours. It suddenly starts to blow and spin in a ferocious wind. I spend some time at the office. Between tidying files and catching up on administrative paperwork that never wanes, I sneak glances out the big windows. I update the website and water the plants. The snow continues to fall. I'm about to head home to pack an overnight bag when the clinking starts against the window.

Sleet. Gray clouds above are still releasing wet snow, but now shards of ice are mixed in. Checking the online weather channel, I see that the city of Burlington and many surrounding areas in Chittenden County are under a severe winter weather advisory. I chew a hangnail, then dial the number for the airline. A mechanical voice tells me that all flights have been canceled. There is as of yet no other information, but I'm encouraged to call back in a few hours and check again. I sigh, visions of desert heat fleeing. After another glance out the window, I decide to call it a day.

I close the office and slip and slide my way to the parking lot behind the building. I pull open the car door. Or, rather, I try to. Ice lays in a thick layer over it. It stings the gap between my coat sleeve and glove. Even after several yanks, a curse, and a smack with my elbow, the handle doesn't budge. I try the one on the hatchback. The big door opens and I crawl over the back seat to retrieve the ice scraper. Feet sticking out of the rear of my Toyota, I imagine what a picture I must make. Cold air and bits of ice bite my calves as I retreat, crawling back out the way I came in.

As though fate has a sense of humor, I hear a low wolf whistle from somewhere nearby. *You've got to be joking.* Cheeks red and irritation boiling in my chest, I ungracefully extract myself the rest of the way and whirl around toward the sound.

A man stands in the shadows nearby, a puffy jacket with a thick hood worn up, shoulders hunched against the wind. He's smoking a cigarette and the burning end makes a tiny glow near his face when he pulls on it.

"Enjoying the show?" I snarl.

"Sorry, I didn't mean to offend you. It's me, Chad."

I peer into the dimness and see the outline of long dreadlocks poking out of the hood of his coat. The anger in my chest cools slightly.

"What do you want?" I ask, turning my back on him and using the handle of the scraper to bang on the driver's side handle. The motion makes my wound ache.

"Just wanted to tell you that Mark is back, that's all." He takes another draw on the cigarette.

I point to the cancer stick. "Aren't you a little health-conscious to be smoking? I thought you were a gym rat."

He sighs, shakes his head, then pulls the cigarette from his mouth and looks at it with disgust. "I know. Can't quit. I've given up meat, most alcohol, and drugs. But these things…" He sighs again. "Man, they're hard to let go."

I hammer at the ice again. Chad walks over and opens his gloved hand and I hesitate before giving him the scraper. It's not that I can't do it myself. But I'm pretty wiped out and my shoulder throbs.

"You saw him?" I ask.

He grunts and whacks at the handle of the door a few times, ice spraying out in glittering shards. When it's free, he jerks it open and motions toward the interior. I climb behind the wheel and crank the engine. It coughs, sputters, and finally turns over. Putting the defrost dial at the highest level, I get out, about to start scraping the windows, but Chad's beat me to it. I'm shivering and my teeth are practically rattling.

"So, when did he get back?" I ask, crossing my arms to retain more body heat.

"Just this afternoon. He stopped by the restaurant, turned in his notice. He's all psyched about this raw food school in Arizona. He's going back in a few days. Just home to get things in order, I guess."

I try to look intrigued rather than guilty that I'd broken into Mark's apartment and had plans to fly to that very location this afternoon.

"Anyway, I just thought you'd want to know." Chad pauses in his scraping and takes a pull on the cigarette dangling from his mouth.

"Thanks," I say.

Chad drops the butt on the ground and stomps it with the toe of his boot, then picks it up and flicks it into the nearby ice-covered bushes. I use the opportunity to snatch the scraper from his hand. He grins at me. "Thanks, I'm getting winded. He's at the billiards club, by the way."

"What, right now?" My breath comes out in big, white puffs as I scrape the last couple of windows. The rearview defroster is doing its work and most of the ice over the hatchback is melting, running in rivulets down the car's body.

"Yeah. I just came from there," Chad says. "He's getting hammered. Celebrating. If you want to talk to him, you might want to go soon." He stretches, looks out toward the road, then back at me. "I'm heading back over if you want to join me."

Since my flight is nonexistent and my trip to sunny Arizona has been canceled, why not?

"Sure," I say. "Want a lift?"

Chad eyes my rust bucket with trepidation.

"Are you sure it will make it?"

"It's three blocks away," I say.

He raises his eyebrows. "I know."

***

The car is still cold when we pull into the billiards club parking lot. It's well-lit, practically blinding with bright street lamps, the sensors misinterpreting the storm for dusk. The club is loud when we enter, music pumping out of miscellaneous speakers above our heads. Chad nods and flicks a peace sign to a beefy guy behind the bar. I follow him to a pool table at the rear where a man is hunched low, lining up for a shot. Another guy sits on a bar stool near the table, rubbing chalk on his cue. He glances our way, nods to Chad, and raises his eyebrows at me. I nod, look back to the man prone over the table. Mark Chester, in the flesh.

He's fit and toned, arm muscles clearly defined through his t-shirt. His jeans don't fit too badly either. Mark makes a good shot, sinking a red ball into the far corner pocket. He stretches to his full height, grins at his stool companion, and then glances toward Chad and me.

"Hey, Chad-O," he says. "Where'd you go?" He snorts a laugh.

Chad smiles but ignores the question.

"This is Tayt Waters. I told you that she'd stopped in to see me at Chantal's."

Mark turns his gaze toward me. His eyes are a blue so bright that they nearly glow. Or maybe it's just the lighting in here. He's attractive: Straight nose, good smile, dark hair that's cut short. He looks like a younger, slightly beefier, and taller version of Tom Cruise.

"How're you doing?" he asks, and walks around the table, holding a hand out to me. I shake it. It's warm and softer than I'd imagined.

"Fine, thanks. Had a good trip?"

Mark inclines his head and Chad says, "I told her you just got back from Arizona."

"It was great, thanks," Mark says to me. "Found my lifelong dream finally, now that I'm in my thirties."

"Better now than never," I say.

Mark smiles and it's crooked. His eyes, I notice, are a little glassy. Chad said he was celebrating.

"Buy you a drink?" Chad asks me.

"Sure. Whatever you're having."

He walks to the bar. I step closer to Mark.

"Is there somewhere private we could talk, just for a

minute?"

Mark glances at the guy on the stool. "Can you give us a few?"

The guy slides off his stool, glares, and follows Chad to the bar.

"This is about as private as it gets here unless you want to follow me to the john," he says.

I smile. "Someone asked me to find you, Mark. Did Chad tell you that?" I ask.

Mark nods. "He said you were asking around about me. Should I be worried?"

"No. At least, I don't think so. But why did you leave without telling anyone where you were going? It's a little weird."

Mark rubs a hand over his face and sighs. "I'll tell you that if you tell me who hired you."

I give a shake of my head. *No, go.*

"What if I were to guess who it was? Would you tell me then?"

I think about this. There's a funny little feeling in the bottom of my brain and it has to do with the missing person report Sandra had filed with the police—Or hadn't filed, as the case may be.

"Okay. Yes," I say.

"Sandra Garrison," Mark says without hesitation.

I nod.

Mark swears and brings his left fist into his right hand. The sound makes a loud thud even over the music and pool balls smacking together. "I can't believe it."

"Well, obviously you can since you knew who it was. Anyway, why wouldn't your girlfriend wonder what happened to you after you left town without a trace? Seems pretty logical to me."

Mark shakes his head. "It's not logical. At all. That's the entire problem with Sandra." His voice is louder as he says, "She lives in a world of make-believe." He waves his hands around his head, enunciating the last two words. "She thinks that I'm her boyfriend. I'm not. She thinks I'm wildly in love with her. I'm not. She thinks that she can stalk me…well, actually, she is stalking me." Mark shakes his head and takes a deep pull from his bottle.

"But…" my voice drifts as I think of evidence to the contrary. Facebook posts—by Sandra only. An unfiled police report. Hiring me to track Mark down and going as far as signing an addendum to our contract for my plane ticket to Arizona.

Signs of a loving girlfriend. And a stalker.

Crap.

Mark is still talking. I give myself a mental shake.

"…when it started. I mean, I liked the girl. She's hot. Really friendly and outgoing. What's not to like, right? But that was before she became a psycho cat woman, sinking her claws into me. Every time I went to the gym, she was there—I don't mean at the desk. I mean there. Following me around, coordinating her routine to mine. She probably would have followed me into the men's locker room if she could have.

"And then there was the great date fiasco." Mark nods to someone behind me and I turn. Chad has reappeared with two bottles of hard cider.

"Want one or are you still working on that?" Chad asks.

Mark shakes his head and takes a longer pull on his bottle of beer.

"So anyway, where was I?" He continues without waiting for a response, "Oh, yeah, date from hell."

Chad makes a sound that is half-snort, half-laugh.

"Let's just say that our first date ended with her in tears because I wouldn't tell her that I loved her and wanted us to get married."

"Wow," I say before I can stop myself.

He nods.

"You can't make up stuff like this." He pauses, looks around the room, and squints. His arms appear suddenly heavy, and he leans against a half-wall, propping himself on it. "She started calling my friends, asking them about me. I caught her more than once outside of my apartment building. She would just sit out there in her car, watching for me.

"It got so bad that I stopped going to the gym for a while. But I'd paid for the year, and I hated to go somewhere else, you know? So, I'd go in when I knew she wasn't working. Except she caught on and started showing up when I was there half the time. She's completely nuts."

Mark pauses to set the empty bottle carefully on the half-wall despite a sign that says, "No bottles or glasses on wall."

"Anyway, I'd been thinking about going out west for a while. I figured, why not now?" He absently rubs a thumb over the label on the beer bottle and it starts to come apart in tiny shreds. "Maybe she helped me, you know? If she hadn't been so persistent, I probably wouldn't have had the balls to do this."

"But why not go to the police?" I ask. I sip my cider and watch for the machoism to emerge. But Mark just shakes his head, looking more like a sad, old dog than a testosterone-filled thirty-something.

"What would be the point? I could have gotten a restraining order, but..." He shrugs. "I don't know. I don't hate her or anything. Anyway, like I said, this ended up pushing me toward something I've been making excuses about for a long time. I guess it's a good thing."

I nod. I can't help but think of my plane ticket. I wonder if I could cash it in for a refund. Or reschedule it and take a little vacation?

"What do you think my chances of getting paid are when I tell Sandra all this?" I'm half-joking.

Chad and Mark glance at each other. Chad raises his eyebrows, and they both laugh.

"As good as a snowball in Ecuador?" I ask.

"Yeah," Mark says, picking up his empty bottle and walking toward the bar. "About that."

Chapter Fifteen

I t's Thursday evening, the sun has just tucked itself into bed, and I'm wishing it was time to roll into my own. Instead, I'm driving back roads in Sheldon, making my way to Prescott's farm in Enosburg. Town lines are screwy in the country; one road might run through three or more different towns, making something as simple as sending a greeting card stress-inducing.

According to Reba, Thursday nights are the one time that Prescott religiously leaves his house. Playing poker is a long-standing tradition. Which works perfectly for me. I chew the inside of my lip, a mix of adrenaline and fear battling in my gut. Flipping through radio channels, I switch from classical to grunge metal, finally settling on reggae. I heard somewhere that reggae helps you calm down, decreasing your heartbeats per minute.

I glance at my roughly drawn map and then look for landmarks: a huge oak on the right, a small knoll, and then, as I crest the hill, a sign for Prescott Acres Farm. It's large and glossy, the spotlight mounted over it nearly blinding. I coast down the knoll and follow Reba's map to a second driveway about a quarter-mile away. It looks like it turns into a field.

I hold my breath. Turning onto it, I pray that my little beater won't get marooned in the deep, frozen, muddy ruts. I follow the driveway—if you can call a narrow strip of mud that—and park near an outbuilding. It's larger than a shed but smaller than a garage. The air is freezing when I open the car door and I shiver.

Grabbing a backpack from the rear seat, I skirt the outbuilding and start walking away from the field, toward the line of trees in the rear. Reba had said that the farmhands would be too busy to gawk outside, but I'm not taking any chances. I also hadn't taken any chances with my appearance, wearing the same garb that I had when I'd met with Reba—makeup, prosthetic nose, and all—on the off chance that someone sees me.

Twigs and fallen branches snap under my boots. The snow is thinner in the woods, though, and, other than avoiding branches to the eye, easy to maneuver. My breath comes in puffy white clouds and the cold snakes its way down into my collar and up around my pant legs. The makeup is itchy.

The woods continue, bordering a cow pasture, but I turn right toward the big, white farmhouse. I can see—and smell—two red barns set some distance away. Cows moo and machines hum. I duck low and run toward the house. Arriving on the rear steps, I make my way up quickly. They spill onto a large, wrap-around porch, typical of many old farmhouses. The porch is chest high and provides a convenient cover.

I crouch down and extract the lock picking kit from my bag. My fingers feel like ice cubes already and I haven't had my gloves off for more than thirty seconds. Blowing warm air on them, I insert the pick into the lock.

On second thought…

I try the door handle. It opens easily in my hand. I grin, feeling a little stupid, and replace my tools in the backpack. Then I use my glove to wipe the door handle where I touched it and push my way into the darkened house.

It's cold inside. It must cost a lot to heat a large house like this, and the drafty, old, single-pane windows don't help. It takes a minute for my eyes to adjust to the dimness inside. I walk into a mudroom, pulling the glove back on. The room is tidy but smells of cows. There are barn boots nearby on rubber mats and smelly clothes hanging on hooks. I move through the room and exit into a large living room. There's a fireplace but no fire lit. The room itself is comfortable but outdated, the shag carpet in dire need of replacement.

A humongous, flat-screen TV is mounted on the wall across from a ratty-looking couch, and beneath the TV, an entertainment center with various black and gray gadgets. I look up and, sure enough, Prescott (or someone he hired) had outfitted the room with surround-sound speakers.

If you were going to spend this much money on making the room into a home theater, wouldn't you replace the nasty carpet first? Maybe upgrade your couch to one without stuffing poking out of the arms?

I leave the living room and pass straight through a dining room and kitchen, both also outdated but clean. When was Leanne here last, I wonder? Just past the kitchen is a set of wide, wooden stairs. I take these and end up in a long hallway filled with many closed doors. Opening the first, I find what seems to be an old sewing room. There are mountains of fabric and two sewing machines on tables opposite each other. I remember Reba saying that Prescott's wife left recently. Must be she hadn't been back to collect her things. Or maybe she wasn't sure it was for good.

A fine layer of dust covers the tables and cabinets and I have a crazy urge to leave a little message in the powdery layer. Or break out a can of Pledge and a rag. I close the door and check the next two rooms, a guest bedroom and what was probably another bedroom at some point but has now morphed into a storage unit. Behind door number four, however, I hit pay dirt: the office.

Prescott breaks all the stereotypes when it comes to farmers; he's obviously very up on technology. There are so many electronic gadgets in the room, it's a wonder he ever has time to do any farm-related things. Say, for instance, milk a cow. But maybe he doesn't.

Pulling off my gloves, I sit gingerly at the desk, slide my backpack to the floor, and wake the dozing computer. It's a PC and the screen, like the television downstairs, is jumbo-sized. Prescott isn't the most organized fellow; there are about fifty icons on the desktop screen, none of which interest me. Instead, I open the Internet browser and check its history. Yesterday's entries were boring: Farm-related, business-related, and one search on toenail fungus.

TMI.

But wait, what have we here? A website called, "sexyromp-ings.com."

I click the site and am treated to more skin than I've seen in the last three Vermont summers put together. I check the history again and find a few more adult sites. Viewing pornography is hardly a crime, though.

My nose feels itchy due to the dust. I do a quick search on the computer's hard drive and find a ton of folders. Like the icons on his desktop, Prescott seems to have files for every document he's ever created or been sent. There is a section that's labeled only with dates. The little arrow hovers over the list.

There is a soft creak from downstairs.

I stop breathing. Is he home from poker early?

Staying where I am, I slouch lower in the high-back office chair and train my eyes to the door. It's located directly across from me, my back vulnerable. Obviously, Prescott is not familiar with the ancient art of Feng Shui, which dictates that when seated in a room, one should always be able to see who is entering and exiting.

Another creak, this time on the stairs. I flick the monitor off and slide out of the chair, moving to the side of the door which is partially closed. My heart is smacking into my ribs, my head yelling, *Run, run, run!* Under the circumstances, though, that seems like a bad choice.

I can barely see through the crack in the door and wiggle a finger through to make the space a little wider. The hallway is dim. I hadn't realized how dark it had gotten outside. Suddenly, I feel eight years old again, having a sleepover at a friend's house. The house is strange and spooky, shadows are throwing unfamiliar shapes around.

Another creak comes, this time from the stairway for sure. *What do I do? What do I do?*

Looking wildly around the room, I notice that no closets or other doors lead into or out of the room. The house must be older than I thought, probably built when armoires were used in place of closets.

There are footsteps now.

I count them: *One, two, three, four, five...*

I grab my stun gun from my coat pocket and try to slow my

breathing down. Attacking Prescott wasn't really on my list of things to do, but what are my other options? On the off chance he doesn't come in here, maybe I can wait him out. If I don't slow my breathing down, though, I'm going to hyperventilate, and then he'll find me in an unconscious puddle on the floor.

Breathe in. Breathe out. Breathe in. Breathe out. When this is over, I promise I'll take up meditation.

The footsteps are still coming up the stairs.

Slow.

Quiet.

A shape appears. It stands at the top of the staircase, motionless.

Chapter Sixteen

T here are no lights on in the hallway—or anywhere else in the house, for that matter. The figure standing there doesn't turn one on.

Because he lives here and doesn't need to, my brain says. *But you don't, so you should get out. Out. Out!*

Believe me, brain, there is nothing I'd like as much.

My breath isn't so loud anymore because I realize I've stopped breathing altogether. I take a few small sips of air and watch as the figure finally moves. It takes a few steps forward, pauses, then stops. Are they listening for something?

I make myself motionless. The slightest change in shadow or variance in light and dark could alert him that I'm here. The shadow moves forward, though, apparently not seeing me. It enters the first bedroom at the top of the stairs. The door creaks when it opens, and the sound reverberates around the still space like a gunshot.

I start breathing again, trying not to pant like a dog.

What was in the first bedroom? I mentally retrace my route. Sewing supplies.

What does Prescott want in there?

Maybe he's a secret seamstress. I have a visual image of

the crusty farm owner bent over one of the sewing machines, humming, straight pins clenched between his lips. Sighing over a crooked seam. Hysterical giggles bubble toward my lips. Inappropriate and uncontrollable laughter is a job hazard.

My thighs ache, my back has a knot from the weird crouched angle I've been standing in. I rise slowly to full height, tuck the stun gun into my pocket, and ease the door open further. A swath of light cuts through the dimness of the hallway, spilling out from the sewing room doorway. I debate with myself, then ease my feet out of toasty boots. I creep slowly along the hallway in my stocking feet.

The floor is cold, the boards slightly rough. Some planks have knots that catch on the fibers of my socks. I stick close to the horsehair plaster walls and pray that none of the boards squeak. Passing the second bedroom, I hear a deep sigh. Not a sigh of sadness or satisfaction, but frustration. Maybe Prescott can't find the right material to finish his quilt? I nearly snort and pinch my nose shut so no sound will escape.

My toes are just about even with the light spilling onto the hallway floor when I hear a voice.

"You've got to be kidding me."

My instinct is to freeze. I've been spotted! But no, the voice sighs again, low and loud. It's coming from the far corner of the room, not near the door. Also, it is not a man's voice, but a woman's.

I press closer to the hallway wall, trying to see through the slit in the open door between the hinges. Mountains of fabric cover nearly every surface. The window opposite me is black, curtains covering it.

A female figure bends over an old desk under the window, opening and closing drawers. She's dressed like me, all in black, but her hair is frizzy and blonde, a mix of ringlets and straw-like pieces poking out wildly from a stocking cap. It must be Prescott's ex-wife. She's small and I breathe a quiet sigh of relief. If there is a confrontation, I can easily take her.

Still, my purpose is to get in and snoop and find something incriminating that I can use against Prescott, not attack his ex. I leave her to her searching and creep back down the hall, trying to find the same spots my feet had touched before.

Nearly back to the office, a board under my left foot squawks like only floors in an old house can. The sound startles me and I jump, then get back into the office and close the door gently.

Crap. Crap. Crap!

The light goes off in the sewing room within ten seconds. Did she fly across the room to hit the lights? I look around the room again, searching for some place to hide.

No closets, my brain reminds me.

The room is crowded with tables and cabinets, but none of them are quite big enough to hide behind and not be seen if the overhead light comes on.

The footsteps near the door. I lunge silently into the space behind the door and have a sudden image of me as a cartoon, smooshed flat into the plaster. The "sleep" button of the computer throws the only light into the room, a faint blue glow.

The door opens silently. I can't see anything, but hear a hand fumbling along the wall, then the bright overhead light glares to life. I have the crazy desire to hide my eyes, as though doing so will keep her from seeing me. Seconds tick by. Convinced that the space is empty, the woman clicks the light switch back off and retreats down the hall.

I would like to say that I immediately bound back to the computer and continue my search like a true professional. But it would be a lie. Instead, I stand rooted in place for about five full minutes, trying to keep from hyperventilating. My heart hasn't experienced this much exertion since before my accident.

Finally, there's a creak in the hallway again, then the sound of footsteps going down the stairs. Seconds later, I hear one of the exterior doors close quietly. I breathe easier knowing I'm alone in the house again.

When I'm calm enough to cross the room, I turn the monitor back on and begin clicking on the files on the hard drive. It's hard to concentrate. I find myself listening for more footsteps or creaks of the floorboards.

Focus.

Okay, where was I? Oh, yeah, the folders are all dated.

I open the first one and my stomach roils. Children in various processes of nudity. I click it closed and open the second to find more. I scroll down quickly and check another date and see more of the same.

The hot, sick feeling in my stomach intensifies. I debate pulling the flash drive from my pocket and copying some of the pictures as evidence. But then what? This isn't an official investigation. How exactly can I tell the cops how I found the evidence?

I think of Reba. If her husband wasn't so desperate for a job… If they could go to the authorities… But they can't. There's no way we can make up a story about Reba finding the pictures, not without them finding out her whole family is working under the table on the farm.

I chew a hangnail as I close out of the folders and go back

to the main screen.

On the one hand, at least I know what I'm dealing with. In addition to mauling Reba's underage daughter, Prescott is a pedophile. But what do I do with this new information? My previous plan—a warning to Prescott—now feels, well, pathetic.

I contemplate my other options. I could:

a) pose as an underage girl online and hope to draw Prescott into meeting with me,

b) wait for him here in the house, where he is unsuspecting, then attempt to kick the crap out of him, or

c) hit on him at a bar or the weekly poker game and try to seduce him into a vulnerable position.

I lean back in the chair. While option "b" is the most attractive to me, let's be honest. Even when I'm at my fighting best and uninjured, attacking a six-foot man with fifty or more pounds on me isn't smart. Yes, I'd have the element of surprise. But that's about my only advantage. There must be something else…

My brainstorming ends abruptly as headlight beams bounce around the room.

He's home.

I jerk upright in the big cushy desk chair and launch myself toward the computer. The plan I came here with will have to do. For now, at least.

Opening the internet browser, I search through Prescott's desk. Although experts tell us to never write down passwords or login information, the gross population ignores this advice. I find the list within a few seconds and practically squeal with happiness. Next, I search Prescott's computer for a headshot. The man likes to appear in the public eye, and it turns out

I have a wealth of options to choose from. I select one that makes his craggy face look smug and save it to the desktop so I can find it easily in a few seconds.

The lights flick off in the driveway and I hear steps stomping up the porch steps. My heart rate skyrockets once again as I hear the door to the house opening, followed by the normal sounds of someone arriving home: boots clunking onto the floor, keys rattling as they bang into something else metal.

I sit motionlessly.

Please, please don't let me pee my pants.

The sound of the TV fills the air. The surround-sound speakers blare. I think of the poor kids on Prescott's computer. Of Leanne. I take a deep breath and continue my work.

Using the password log, I go into the first of his social network accounts, Facebook, and log in. Prescott has been busy, happily updating his status to reflect all the good he's been doing in schools and nonprofits around the county.

I start a new post on his timeline.

"I'm ashamed to admit this, but there is something that has been eating away at me, something I can't keep secret anymore. I'm a pedophile. After all these years it feels good to get this off my chest."

I hit return and watch the status update. After doing the same on each of his social networking sites, I open another window and create a phony email account for Prescott in two minutes. Then I write a long, poignant letter about the fact that he can't stand the lies anymore, that he's officially coming out of the closet and admitting that he is a sexual predator. The television downstairs continues to blare. It sounds like he's watching an episode of CSI or another crime show.

Fitting.

I upload his smug photo as an icon on his account, then send the email off to the news desk at three local papers. I'd jotted the newspapers' email addresses on a scrap of paper which I retrieve from my back pocket. I have no idea if they'll run with it or not, but at least I've planted a seed.

Now for the best part.

Logging into a free, online photo editing program, I upload Prescott's picture one more time, add in text about his love of underage porn, and enlarge the photo. It looks cheesy and homemade, but it will serve its purpose.

I check the printer for paper and am happy to see that the man has not just regular-sized but jumbo sheets for his oversized office printer. I make the necessary adjustments and send ten of the flyers to the printer. Holding my breath, I wait for the printer. The volume of the TV is cranked so loudly, though, that I don't need to worry about Prescott hearing anything up here.

Clicking back onto the Facebook window, I see a steady stream of insults already building under the recent update. Some posters are confused: "Is this a joke?" Others are hurling obscenities right and left.

I grin, log out of all the open windows, and go to the computer's history button, deleting all my recent online activities. While it's shutting down, I pull a little card from my pocket. It's about the size of a drink coaster and blank, except for a butter-yellow sunflower in the bottom corner. In large, block letters I print the words, "Stay away from Leanne" and sign it, "A friend."

Turning the computer off, I hear the printer spitting out the last paper. At the same time, I hear something else.

Silence.

It's as loud as the television was minutes ago, quietness pressing against my eardrums and smothering me. Grabbing the flyers, I shove them between my shirt and jacket, rub the edge of my flannel shirt over the keyboard, printer, and everything else I remember touching in a clumsy attempt to erase myself from the room. I turn off the computer and printer and pocket the pen I'd used—the gel ones are my favorites. Then, slipping my backpack straps over my shoulders, I walk in stocking feet back to the hall.

The television clicks back on. Maybe he was just making a phone call or something. The volume is a bit lower now, though. I stand, shivering, in the hall.

Where are my boots? I turn. Grabbing them in one hand, I steady myself on the wall. The TV turns off again and I hear footsteps on the floor beneath me. I can't put the boots on now. The sound of clunking overhead is sure to alert him of my presence.

Or is he already aware?

Another creak of floorboards, and then the sucking sound of the fridge door opening, a bang when it shuts. The TV is still off. Why keep turning it on and off?

Creeping down the hall in the opposite direction of the staircase, I pray not to hit any squeaky floorboards. My mouth is pasty. When I run my tongue over my lips, it practically sticks.

I pass another darkened bedroom, then there is an expanse of the hall without doors. Finally, at the end, is the entryway where I'd come up the stairs.

I reach out to grasp the railing when, suddenly, behind me, footsteps thunder up another flight of stairs at the opposite end of the hall. Light floods the hallway.

I'm caught.

Chapter Seventeen

I jerk the door before me open.

At the same time, a deep voice yells, "Hey!"

Heart skittering, I race down the second staircase two at a time. Footsteps thunder down the hallway and I slip, nearly falling, as I miss the last step.

The staircase spits me into the kitchen and I run through the living room and out of the exterior door where I first came in. The posters in my shirt are itchy, but I clamp one arm across my stomach to keep them from falling out. My boots are still in my hand. I don't have time to stop and put them on.

Feet pound behind me. Another low curse.

I launch myself down the front stairs and start running across the field to my car. Hopefully, Prescott also has no shoes on. My boots are sliding in my free arm, my feet feel like ice cubes. If I glance down, I'm sure I would see puffy snow slippers over my socks. My breath comes in big clouds of white. I slip, nearly twist an ankle in a divot in the field. I glance behind me and see no one. I slow my stride but keep moving, twisting my head behind me and searching wildly.

Nothing.

I stop, gasping for air, and turn around completely. There!

Just coming out of the house, pulling the last boot on, is Prescott. Do I have time to put on my own?

No.

I run again. Where is the shed? Seconds later I crest a small knoll and see the nose of my ancient Toyota silhouetted in the darkness. Thank God for the full moon. I put on a final burst of speed, a side stitch threatening to stop my breath altogether. I grab the driver's side handle. The door squeals in protest, the sound cutting through the silence of the cold winter night.

Launching myself behind the wheel, I don't even bother to remove the posters. My feet are so cold that I feel nothing below my ankles. Hopefully, I will be able to feel the gas pedal.

The car starts on the first try (miracle!) and I slam the shifter into reverse and bounce back down the snow-covered dirt driveway for a few seconds. A spot on my left widens where a tractor would have room to navigate into the field. I back the car in, put it into first gear. Flick on the lights and slam my foot on the gas. Snow spins off the back tires. I glance in the rearview mirror and see a shadow standing at the top of the knoll, then running toward me.

Bouncing and jerking, the car finally finds its way to the main road, and I spin out of the driveway.A scream—half laughter, half relief—erupts from my lips.

Grinning like I won the lottery, I can't stop laughing.

I did it!

I'm still smiling three miles down the road when blue lights appear in the rearview mirror. I've had nightmares about this: When a cop pulls me over and my driver's license looks nothing like my disguise. Making matters worse, I'm still bootless and have evidence of my recent crime stuck up the front of my shirt. My heartbeat, which had just started to return to normal, starts to race again.

Could Prescott have called it in? But that doesn't make any sense—he wouldn't want to get the authorities involved.

I steer to the side of the road and smooth a hand over my wig, tugging it back into place. Should I take it off? But then what can I do about the theater makeup and prosthetic nose? There's a knock on my window and I roll it down, smiling. Hopefully a nice, normal-looking smile—not like a maniac.

"Good evening, ma'am," a voice says from behind a blinding flashlight.

"Hello, officer," I say back, fiddling with a button on my shirt.

The cop readjusts the angle of the light so that it's not shining into my eyes and I can see him slightly better. He is young with light eyes and a bad complexion.

"Do you know why I stopped you?"

What to say, what to say?

"Because I was breaking and entering?" or *"For defamation?"*

Instead, I shake my head. "Not really."

"You were speeding."

I want to laugh out loud in delight. *Speeding? Is that all? Wonderful!*

"Sorry, officer," I say. "It's late and I'm tired. I didn't realize…
"

"License and registration, please."

I dig in the glove box and extract the registration and reach for my wallet, which is buried under the front passenger seat, to get my license out.

Handing both to him, I motion to my face.

"You might notice that I don't look like my picture. I'm in a play and we were practicing tonight."

"What's the name of it?"

"Sorry?"

"The play. What is the name of it?" he repeats the words more slowly and loudly, as though I'm stupid. I'm starting to wonder that myself.

"Oh, uh, it's *Our Town.*"

"Never heard of it," he says. "You get all dressed up in makeup and"—he glances at my license again—"a wig…for practice?"

"Oh, yes." I put what I hope is an excited-bordering-on-thrilled note into my voice. "It helps me to get in character."

He frowns, nods.

"Sit tight," he says and walks back to his cruiser.

My palms are so sweaty, I'm surprised the documents hadn't flown to the ground when I'd handed them over. Do I have any skeletons in my driving closet as of late? I go through my mental files. It's been at least a year since I've gotten a speeding ticket. Parking violations? *Please, please, please don't ask me to get out of the car for any reason.* I consider putting my boots on but figure rummaging around under my seat might look a little suspicious, or at the very least, draw attention. How long before frostbite sets in? My toes are still numb, and I crank the heat dial up. The pathetic stream of warm air that comes out is like that from a newborn's mouth.

My teeth chatter. This could be because the window is still half-open or just good ole' nerves. I crank the window closed in case it's the former and sit on my hands. Warmth returns to my fingertips after a couple of long minutes. What's he doing back there? Playing a few rounds of Candy Crush while I freeze to death? Maybe he's trying to wait out my guilty conscience.

Finally, I hear the crunching of his boots on snow and roll

my window back down halfway. I smile up at him, feel the prosthetic nose pulling against my skin and itching.

"All set?" I ask in a sweet, hopefully innocent-sounding voice.

"You were traveling sixty in a fifty-mile-per-hour zone," he says and hands my paperwork through the window. "I'm letting you off with a warning this time, but please, don't make me regret my decision."

"Thank you. I won't. Make you regret it, I mean. I'll be a model driver, promise." I smile again and this time part of the nose pulls free. It smells like a tire but is officially the only part of my body that's warm.

"Be careful out there," he says, and heads back to his cruiser.

I want to pump my fist enthusiastically in the air but refrain. Instead, I carefully check behind me (as if not doing so would cause a pile-up on this deserted road), apply my blinker like a good citizen, and pull back out onto the road. I drive forty-five (just to be safe) for the next five miles, then pull onto the side of the road again, get out, and put the icy lumps I used to call feet into my boots.

Ten minutes later, I follow signs into the village of Enosburg and plaster four of the signs onto public bulletin boards. An hour after that, I've deposited the rest of the posters on boards in Richford, Sheldon, and a couple in St. Albans for good measure.

My feet have thawed to the point of throbbing when I finally pull into my driveway. Twenty minutes later, in front of a small electric heater, they are finally beginning to feel like feet again, instead of giant toothaches. I'm sipping a glass of wine, imagining Prescott's reaction to his newfound fame.

It's nearly eleven o'clock when the house phone rings. I

stagger out of my chair.

The smile vanishes when I hear the voice on the other end of the phone.

"I'm going to hurt you…" It's the same strange, mechanical voice.

I slam the receiver back into its cradle and, when it starts ringing again seconds later, pull the cord from the wall.

Chapter Eighteen

My heart is hammering as I walk into the kitchen for a glass of cold water. I drink it, then check locks on the front door and the window latches with shaking fingers, making sure all are closed tight. Stupid, I know. It was likely just some teenager making prank calls. Still, when I crawl into bed a half-hour later, I'm reassured by the Glock under the pillow next to me.

***

The next morning dawns bright and clear, sunshine jamming its way under my sleepy eyelids. I roll over and look at the clock. It's after nine.

Showering quickly, I pour myself a travel mug of green tea and go through all the normal pre-work, morning routines: turning down the thermostat, wiping counters, and checking my cell phone for any messages. The signal is surprisingly good this far out. It's probably time to let go of the landline phone. Thinking of the call last night, I shiver.

The sun bounces off the snow-covered road, nearly blinding me as I crest the hill leaving Hendricks Falls. I adjust and readjust the visor, then finally give up. I'm too short for it to be effective. Instead, I use my hand to block the light until I'm far enough down the hill that it's not an issue. I see a couple of trucks and one SUV on my way to St. Albans, otherwise, the road remains deserted.

I should walk over to Winston's tonight. My neighbor, a few seeds short of a full packet, is in his sixties and spends most of his time fixing mechanical things and preparing for *The Dark Times* which he's convinced will soon be upon us. Despite this viewpoint, he's a pretty happy guy, and even though his place is like a hoarder's-paradise-meets-WWII-bunker, he's become a sort of father figure to me. I haven't seen him in over a week, though. I worry about him up there all alone without a telephone. Tonight, I'll bring him dinner.

Grabbing a local paper at the coffee shop on Main Street, I see a front-page headline: "Prescott Acres Farm Owner, Emerson Prescott, Accused of Child Pornography."

I pay for a coffee, a pastry, and the paper without even looking at the barista, my eyes already scanning the article. There's a shot of one of my posters, blown up big. An article starts to the right. I grin as I read:

"The image of local philanthropist and farmer, Emerson Prescott, was seen in town today on posters (as seen on the left) accusing him of being involved in child pornography. Prescott, who sits on several educational and town planning boards, has not yet been reached for comment. Since the posters were discovered earlier this morning, several town residents have already come forward to share their opinions.

"Edith Wardell, a long-time resident of Enosburg, states that whoever created the posters should be 'ashamed of themselves.' This reaction was not shared by Judith Rainville. 'Prescott had this coming. My daughter was involved in one of his programs at the school and said that he gave her the creeps. We can't allow people like this to run loose in our communities, in our schools. Something should be done about him and all the other pedophiles.'

"It's unclear as to who created or distributed the posters late last night. Could it be a prank? Wardell believes so.

'Whoever did this is just trying to make trouble, trying to damage the name of a wonderful man and a great asset to our community here in Franklin County.'"

I read a few more lines, basically the reporter stating that anyone with information about who might have created the posters should please get in touch with the editorial office and/or the police station immediately. The reporter pointed out the fact that the newspaper has no opinion on the subject but is objectively reporting on community news. (In other words, covering their hineys.)

Practically skipping to my car, I can't keep a smile from my face. It's not often that true justice is served or crimes against the innocent are prevented. This is the sole reason for Sunflower Specials. Well, that, and the money, of course. I'm not a mercenary by any definition, but the pile of hospital bills and my passion for fashion have to be taken care of somehow.

So far, no sugar daddy has volunteered to take on the job.

When I get to the office, I spend a few minutes piddling around with email and going through the real paper mail before checking for phone messages. Someday I'd love to hire an assistant to take care of all this for me. At present, though, I'm the accountant, marketing director, receptionist, and every other staff member that a typical business requires.

There's a message from Phil about our "date" and I glance at the calendar, groaning. Seriously? My good mood evaporates like mist from a can of aerosol hairspray. How did I forget that tonight is the night of the big anniversary party? And here I was hoping to spend a quiet evening with my buddies Ben & Jerry. I make a note to call Phil back. We're supposed to go over the details (i.e. lies) of how we met, what we like to do together, if we have any annoyingly babyish names for each other—you know, the things normal, dating people have already worked out.

There's one other message, this one from Sandra Garrison. I groan again. In my adrenaline-infused state, I'd forgotten temporarily about her and Mark and the whole stalker issue.

Good luck getting paid for this one, my nasty inner voice says.

I could put her off. There's a ton of paperwork to do. I haven't had time to finish all the website updates I wanted to. And, honestly, I'd rather pluck my eyebrows, get a root canal, *and* go swimsuit shopping than make this call. But I force myself to dial her cell phone. It rings three times before Sandra answers.

"It's Tayt," I say. "We need to meet."

∗∗∗

I secure a table, once again, at Juice Bar. Where Sandra was model-glimmery the last time we'd met, this time I barely recognize her. She slouches through the door, hair unkempt and straggly around her face. She's wearing workout clothes, but none of the form-fitting lycra and spandex. This time it's baggy sweatpants and a gray track jacket with white strips up the arms. Her face is makeup-less and her eyes are rimmed pink.

I wave to her from the small table, the bright lights making me wish I'd brought sunglasses. Sandra walks over, collapsing onto a stool at the high table.

"Everything okay?" I ask.

She shrugs, nods, then shakes her head, *no.*

I've debated asking her what's wrong. I'm not her therapist and from the look of the woman, it's going to be a long story. Still, my gut tells me to do the right thing.

"Want to talk about it?"

She shrugs and looks at her hands, which are resting on the table as though they are unfamiliar to her. Rubbing one finger absently, she surveys the room, then glances toward me.

"I just get like this sometimes." Her voice is low, so quiet that I lean forward to hear. "It's like a sort of depressed state. I don't know." She shrugs. "My therapist tried putting me on some meds, but they made me feel so"—she shrugs again—"out of it. Numb. It was like I was living underwater. So, I stopped taking them."

"How long does it last?"

She rubs her hands over her face, and then leaves them there, talking to me through them. "A while. Days, sometimes. A week or two at most. I'll be fine."

We sit like this for a few minutes, me watching Sandra and

alternately scanning the room as people come and go. Sandra just has her hands over her face.

Finally, I ask, "Can I get you something?"

She shakes her head.

"Look, I have to get back to the office," I say, feeling rude. But seriously, is my sitting here helping her? "I wanted to talk to you about Mark."

She lifts her head at this, hands dropping to the table with a *thunk.*

"He's back in town, isn't he?" she asks.

I nod. "He is. I saw him at the billiards hall and he told me something a little…" How to put this? "Disturbing."

Sandra stares at me, eyes vacant. It's like looking into an abyss. How far down does the emptiness go? She doesn't say anything, so I go on.

"He told me that you guys weren't dating. That he only knows you from the gym." I think, in all honesty, I've done a good job at being diplomatic here. I didn't blurt out what I've been thinking—*He thinks you're a psychopathic stalker*—after all.

"Yeah, well, he would say that." Her words are clipped. Sarcastic.

"What do you mean?"

"Just that he's a typical man. All hot to get into my pants, but now that he's done, he's ready to toss me out with the trash. What, does he think that I will just shut my mouth and take it?" She bites off these last words so savagely I half-expect her teeth to snap together. She rubs her hands together twice, then pinches the skin over her knuckles tightly between her finger and thumb. It turns pink, then white.

"Look, I don't want to get in the middle of whatever it is

that's going on here," I say. "I heard a very different story from Mark, but it's not my job to choose sides. As a professional courtesy, I wanted to give you an update, and—"

"Gee, thanks. I appreciate your concern."

I sigh and rub my fingers over my jawbone. Patience is a virtue. One I lack.

"Whatever you do from here is your call. I'm just telling you that I'm out of this. Here's the bill for services rendered." I slap the white carbon sheet on the table. "Any questions, my office number is on the bottom of the invoice."

I stand up. Sandra gazes past my shoulder, her eyes filling with tears.

"I'm sorry that it didn't work out the way you'd hoped," I say more gently. "It sucks when someone you love doesn't feel the same about you."

She chuckles—a rough, dusty sound—and roughly slashes her hands across her eyes. "Doesn't it, though?" she says.

I leave her sitting at the table, hands once again cradling her head.

Chapter Nineteen

At two o'clock, I meet with Phil at another café on Main Street. Funky artwork and little plaques reminding coffee drinkers of the health benefits of drinking joe line the walls. He approaches me, thankfully, because I probably would have sat there for a good half-hour waiting for him to show up in his goth-wear.

"Tayt?" he says, walking toward me with his hand extended. "You look great. It's been a while, hasn't it?"

I stumble over my first few words, surprised to see that Phil-the-grownup looks nothing like Phil-the-Pill. He is no longer sporting a head of shaggy hair dyed black or the multiple piercings and eyeliner that I remember. Instead, he is clean-shaven, has medium brown hair and brown eyes free of makeup. He's dressed in khakis, a light blue button-down shirt, and a pair of red Converse sneakers. He's also got a cool-looking belt, which looks like it's made from pieces of broken CDs.

"Oh. Uh, yeah, I guess it has." I smile.

He smiles back. "I look a little different, huh?"

I nod, cheeks red. Were my thoughts that obvious? Ezra always says that I have a "feeling face," meaning that whatever

I'm feeling is written directly across my face.

"Join me?" he asks, motioning toward the table where he'd been sitting.

I trail behind him, hopping onto the tall stool and surveying the area while Phil goes to get us coffees. There are two mothers alternately chasing giggling toddlers to the front door and plopping them back at their tables. A harried barista waits on a line of customers five people deep, Phil the last in line.

Finally, he returns, two stoneware mugs of coffee steaming. I accept mine gratefully and stir in cream and sugar. Phil drinks his black.

"So, where do we start?" he asks.

"Well. With the details, I guess," I say. I'm glad he's not interested in a lot of small talk. "We should go over what our likes/dislikes are, how we met, what traits about you annoy me, that type of thing."

He cocks an eyebrow at the last bit.

"What about the traits about you that annoy *me?*" he jokes.

"Oh, Phil. You have a lot to learn about me. The first is that you're head over heels for me and *nothing* I do irritates you."

He grins.

"I knew I hired the right woman to be my girlfriend."

***

Ezra calls that night just as I'm putting the finishing touches on my makeup for the party.

"Going out?" he asks, probably noting my breathless "I'm-nearly-late-once-again" voice.

"Yeah, I have that party tonight. Remember, with Phil?"

"Phil-the-Pill? Oh, yeah, I remember." He chuckles and I

seriously consider slamming the receiver down.

"Funny. I'm running late. Can I call you back later?"

He's quiet for a moment. I pull the phone away from my ear. Did I lose the call? But then his voice comes back on the line.

"Sure, it's no big deal. I'm just, you know, considering a huge life change and seeking counsel from family and friends. But no big deal," he says again, sighing dramatically. I can hear the laughter behind it, though. "Whenever you have time to fit me in, give me a ring."

"Oh, for pity's sake! We can talk while I'm on the road."

"No, that's okay," he says. "I'm kidding. I mean, I do want your advice on something, but there's no rush. Have fun tonight," he says, "on your date." He laughs again, which turns into a snort.

When I say something rude into the receiver and hang up, Ezra is still chuckling.

Hardy-har-har. Tayt gets herself into the most ridiculous situations...

***

I meet Phil at the Hannaford shopping plaza on Shelburne Road. The wind is whipping when I leave my Toyota and I worry that all the hard work on my hair will be undone before I make it the ten steps to Phil's Mercedes.

Wait, a Mercedes? Doesn't the man work as a telemarketer?

"Hey, glad you made it. You look fantastic, Tayt," Phil says as I slide into my seat. The cushion under my bum is toasty and the interior smells like cologne. Good cologne. Expensive. Not that cheesy stuff they sell at the local drugstore.

"Thanks. Nice car," I say, hoping that he'll tell me how he

affords it.

"Yeah. A gift from my parents."

I raise my eyebrows.

"Wow. That's quite a gift."

"Mmm, it is. I get a new one every Christmas."

I have no response to this and just sit there, blinking.

"They're still holding on to the hope that I'll rise to a career in which it makes sense to own a car like this, like a banker or a lawyer. They've given up the dream of a career in medicine. I'm too squeamish."

"But you work in, uh, marketing?"

"Just now, to pay the bills. My fiancée and I have a side business together. Had," he corrects himself. "It's not bringing in a lot of money yet, but someday I hope to do it full-time." Phil glances at me. "Promise you won't laugh."

"Okay," I say, biting my tongue as a preventative measure.

"It's a photography business where I take glamour shots of people's pets."

"Oh?" I manage.

"It's great," Phil says and motions with his hands as he describes the bathing, grooming, and manicures (or maybe "paw-icures" would be a better word?) that he gives each animal before "…staging them, like a real Hollywood photo shoot."

"That's…interesting," I say, unsure how else to respond. "Do the pets like it?"

"For the most part. They like pampering, just like humans. The treatments are very relaxing and the final effect…well, you'd have to see the photos yourself to fully understand. Their owners are overjoyed. We offer packages at different levels, depending on the number of poses and props that the customer wants. And of course, how the pet takes to the process."

"Oh, of course," I say. "So, you do that around here?" I can't imagine anyone in the state being interested. Most communities are made up of hard-working, dyed-in-the-wool types where "dressing up" means wearing something other than flannel and jeans. But maybe I've just been hanging out in the wrong crowd. The one that doesn't get a new Mercedes gifted to them each Christmas.

"No. Well, not yet. I'm based in Burlington—that's where I live—and have a room in our…sorry, my apartment converted for the studio." Phil speeds up on the interstate and I watch the dark trees flashing past the windows.

We drive in silence for a few minutes and then Phil makes a left, following winding routes until we reach his parents' house. It's large, a contemporary monster built of stone and steel and wood beams. The pea stone driveway is circular and there are cars parked in a second area off the circle. Lexus, BMWs, and Audis fill the area. I think of my rusty Toyota and grin. Imagine showing up in that! The other vehicles would surely shudder in embarrassment.

The air outside the house is cold, an icy wind blowing across the open meadow behind the house and circling the front. It whips my coat against my bare legs and tugs at the scarf around my neck. I hold onto it with one hand and Phil guides me to the front entrance, his hand on my back. He's picking right up on this "young couple in love" thing. I'm praying I don't trip and faceplant in the doorway.

A woman with a dark, sleek bob opens the door. She's pencil-thin, her skin pulling tightly against collarbones that would petrify any baby looking for a cuddle. Her dress is as long and narrow as she is, some dark color that I can't make out in the low light.

"Darling," she says, pressing her face against Phil's. The door closes behind us and I hear low, classy jazz in some other room, the tinkle of glassware, and murmured voices.

"Mother, this is Ashley," Phil says, pulling away from his mother's claw-like hands. She pulls back and looks at me, but her fingers stay, grazing Phil's arm in a way that says, *"mine."*

I smile, pray that I don't have any lunch bits left between my teeth, and say, "What a beautiful home you have. It's a pleasure to meet you." I hold out a hand, but she ignores it, instead pressing her fingers into her son's arm.

"Everyone is waiting to see you," she says, pouting, and motions toward another room down a wide hallway. I stand there for a second, hand outstretched stupidly, before letting it fall to my side. For a minute I feel like that kid in grade school that no one wants to sit with at lunchtime.

Phil is no help; he's already heading off down the hall. With a mother like that, no wonder Phil doesn't date.

"Sorry about that," a man's voice says from behind me. "Vivian is very protective of her little boy."

I turn, see a man in his late 60s swirling amber-colored liquid in a short glass. "I'm Philip's father, Jacob."

I grasp his outstretched hand, which is warm, and give it a firm shake. "Let me take your coat." He deposits it into a wide hall closet.

"Can I get you a drink?" he asks.

"Sure, thanks," I say. "Whatever you're having."

"This is thirty-year-old scotch."

"Sounds great."

He nods in approval and ducks back into the room, a kitchen

I realize as I follow him in.

"So, you're Ashley. We haven't heard a lot about you, I'm sorry to say." Jacob says this not unkindly. I lean against a stainless-steel fridge (that probably costs as much as my office rent for the year) and smile.

"But it's good to see him dating again. After...well."

I thank him for the drink he hands me and take a small sip. It burns like lava in my esophagus.

"So," I search my mind for some neutral ground. "Are you a—"

"Darling, what are you doing in here? Our guests miss you," Vivian's voice interrupts. She's returned to drag her seemingly-normal-compared-to-her husband out of my vicinity. What is it with this woman? Could she be any ruder? I draw myself up to my full height plus four inches (thanks to my spindly heels) and smile at her.

"Jacob and I were just talking about Phil," I say brightly. "And he made me a drink." I hold it aloft as though to prove I'm not lying. Vivian barely glances in my direction. Instead, she grabs her husband's bicep and starts to propel him through the doorway.

I trail along behind, like an errant dog.

We arrive in the great room—because really, a room this size is way too big to be called a living room—to find Phil in the center of a small group of people his parents' age. All are chuckling and smiling at him in appreciation. Phil laps up the attention like a show pony.

"...I meant what I said," he says, finishing the recounted story, complete with hand gestures. The group laughs again, a couple of the women closest to him drawing near enough to pat his cheek or arm as though reassuring themselves that it's really, truly Phil in the flesh, not just an apparition.

Good grief.

The group starts to chat among themselves once again, except for one older lady who still has her arm locked through Phil's as he turns toward his parents and me. I stand slightly behind them and try to look perturbed. I mean, I am supposed to be his girlfriend. Polite guys don't just ditch their sweethearts the moment they walk into their parents' home, right?

I hear the front door close and heels clicking on the hallway floor, and I glance in that direction. Vivian is already halfway to that side of the room, holding her stick arms out in front of her, ready to embrace…oh, no.

A woman that I very much don't want to see stands in the doorway.

Chapter Twenty

I don't think I ever learned the woman's name from the house party in Colchester. I just refer to her in my head as "Hippie Skank." Tonight, rather than a flowing dress and half-done braids, she is dressed to the nines and towers over Vivian. She squeals in what can only be described as joy and leans in for a strange air-hug. I turn away slightly to avoid eye contact. My palms immediately dampen. Jacob notices my reaction, or more likely the grimace on my face, and misinterprets it.

"Are you feeling ill?" he asks.

"What? Oh, uh, just a little lightheaded. I think I might need some air."

"That's a strong drink if you don't usually imbibe," he says, and nods, pointing across the room to a glass door. I hadn't noticed it blending in with a wall of windows.

"Thanks," I say and head in that direction.

Phil is still in the clutches of the older woman, who continues to pat his arm and smile up at him. I veer in that direction.

"We've got a problem," I hiss, drawing close to his ear. Phil laughs and nods and I want to deck him. Then I realize he's just acting as though I told him something flirtatious.

"I can't explain right now, but that woman who just walked in…" I wait for Phil to nod, which he does. "I'll tell you outside. Meet me, okay?" I say in his ear. I can't explain any further because Vivian's heels are chipping away at the stone floor behind me. I walk more quickly to the door, fanning myself with my hand and smiling politely at anyone making eye contact.

The icy air takes my breath away and I immediately start shivering. The thin dress feels like it's made of paper. I long for my coat. Big puffs of white cloud my vision momentarily, but I continue walking around the side of the house to a spot in the shadows. I stand for a few seconds, staring in at the group of guests. It feels like a Christmas card come to life, all glittery lights, hors d'oeuvres on silver platters, thin-stemmed glasses, and—

"Want a smoke?" a voice asks.

It's so close to my ear that I jump and whirl around, hands automatically going up into protective mode.

"Whoa," the voice says. "I know smoking is unhealthy, but I doubt you'll get cancer from one cigarette. And I promise I'm not going to light you on fire or anything."

The voice is male, and I can make out the shadow of a figure, but no features.

"What…" ("*Chatter, chatter, chatter,*" go my teeth.) "What are you doing?" *Chatter chatter.*

"Here, take my coat," the voice says, and long arms move in my direction. I dance backward (not an easy feat in these heels) and say, loudly, "Hey!"

"Shhh." The arms stop mid-motion. "I'm Chris. Phil's cousin."

"You"—*chatter, chatter*—"are?"

"Uh-huh. I can't believe he didn't tell you about me," he sounds slightly offended. "But I am the black sheep of the family, so I guess it makes sense."

I think of Vivian. If I were related to her, I'd be the black sheep, too.

I make a disgruntled noise but accept the coat. It's warm as toast on my frigid skin and smells like a bottle of cologne had been spilled on it. I pull it close anyway and murmur a thank you.

"So," I say. "Did you know Phil's fiancée?"

Chris nods. "Mary? Yeah, we used to hang out together, a foursome. Me and my wife Cindy." He points with his cigarette toward a woman standing near a grand piano. "We spent a lot of time with them."

"You know, Phil doesn't like to talk about her. About Mary," I say. "But I wondered how long it's been since she, uh, passed on."

"Mary?" Chris takes a deep drag, the orange glow lighting his face momentarily. "It's been, what, seven years now? No, eight. I forgot that it was when Mary was pregnant with our second kid."

Eight years? I want to ask him to repeat himself. No wonder his parents have been wanting Phil to start dating again.

I move further into the shadows and reposition myself so that the light from the windows isn't blinding me anymore. Chris is medium height and husky and looks uncomfortable in his suit. He pulls at the collar as though reading my mind.

"So why are you out here?" he asks finally.

"I saw a—" I stop myself before I say, "client." "Someone inside I'd rather not run into."

"Oh. That describes more than half of the people in there,"

Chris takes another drag, the smoke making a white wreath over his head.

"It's complicated," I say. "I'm not sure how I'm going to get through the rest of the evening without her seeing me, though."

"Is she a brunette and tall with killer gams?" Chris asks, facing the bank of windows.

"Yes. How did you—"

"I don't think you'll have to worry about her recognizing you in a few minutes. She just sucked down a glass of champagne like it was water and she was in a marathon. And now she's working on a glass of something brown. Might be bourbon." He pauses for another drag on the cigarette. Seconds later he says, "Oh. That's half-gone, too."

"Good. I should have worn a disguise," I say.

Chris laughs at this. As if I were kidding.

I wait another five minutes and then reluctantly pull off the coat and hand it back. "Thanks for letting me borrow this. I should go back in. How does she look now?"

Chris checks the windows.

"I'd say you're good to go. She's propped up on a houseplant and waving her arms around."

"Great. Drunks are much easier to deal with and tend to be non-credible, so I should be safe." My teeth have started rattling together again. "Thanks again for the coat. See you inside?" *Chatter, chatter.*

"Yeah, I'll be in shortly." Chris sounds like he's facing a death sentence. He gives me a two-finger salute and shrugs the jacket back on.

I nod and heave a sigh, heading back to the glass door and the warmth and loud awkwardness of a party where I don't know anyone.

Time to double my rates.

***

The party lasted until the wee hours of the morning. Conversation and laughter flow more easily as the hours, and booze, ran. I guess the plethora of cosmetics applied did the trick in making me look somewhat different. Hippie Skank, luckily, hadn't recognized me. She'd mentioned twice during dinner that I looked "so familiar," but someone always interrupted her line of thinking with a question about her family or job.

In the end, the night was a success, at least in Phil's eyes. He was so grateful that he gave me a two-hundred-dollar tip. I thanked him and offered to be his fill-in girlfriend whenever needed.

***

My bedroom is ice cold when I wake up. I stumble to the living room and check the thermostat while shivering. My teeth chatter together like a chipmunk on speed. I rub my hands over my arms, stomping my feet simultaneously.

The gauge reads fifty-two degrees. Surprisingly, I can't see my breath. When I call my friendly fuel company they say they'll see what they can do.

"See what you can do? I'm literally freezing here."

"Well, ma'am, we have a lot of heating issues to deal with today. I'll get someone out to see you just as soon as I can," says a nasally woman on the other end of the phone who sounds anything but concerned. Why would she be, sitting in a toasty-warm office?

"That'd be great, seeing as soon all the pipes are going to burst and I'm going to have to sue you for negligence. I believe one of your technicians was out here, what was it, three weeks ago, to clean the furnace?" I hear something on the other end. Is she eating something? "And now it's not working. At all," I say, voice growing louder. "So yeah, if you can squeeze me in, that would be great."

There is a noisy clearing of the throat on the other end of the phone.

"As I said, I'll see what I can do. Was there anything else you needed assistance with today?"

"Can you just try to get this one thing right?" is what I want to respond. But instead, I take a big, deep breath (difficult, since my lungs are sprouting icicles) and say, "No, thank you. That's all."

I debate leaving the house unlocked for the service guy since I have no idea when he'll show up and I have a crap-load of work to do at the office. Plus, despite the extra layers I've piled on, I'm still cold. But I decide to stay.

I call my office phone remotely to check messages. It says there are two. The first is from the hospital billing office. *Delete.* The second is from a woman who says her name is Molly Stevens. Molly needs my services but doesn't give any details. She sounds young and pretty. I picture blonde curls and big, blue eyes.

Another relationship issue?

Groan.

***

It's two o'clock when I finally get into the office. The heating technician had tried to explain what was wrong, but he must have noticed my eyes crossing. Finally, he said, "And you're all set. Have a good day!" and left me with an invoice. I shove it into a drawer with a bunch of other unpaid bills. Someday soon I'm going to have to deal with those.

I'd connected with Molly over the phone and, since I didn't have anything scheduled for this afternoon, we agreed to meet. She'll be here in a half-hour or so. I spend the time sipping a cup of extra hot coffee, rifling through both snail mail and email.

A knock sounds on the door at precisely two-thirty and a young woman pushes it open. My mental picture was spot on. Goose bumps pop up on my arms; I should hire myself out as a psychic.

Molly is about five foot five, a little plump, and well-dressed with short blond curls. On me, it would look clownish, but on her it's striking. She has on a shade of red lipstick that makes me think of flappers in the 20s. Stylish. Pretty. I introduce myself, offer her a chair and cup of coffee, tea, or water, but she refuses them all so we get down to business.

Molly clears her throat, but when she starts to speak her voice breaks like a thirteen-year-old boy's. She clears it again and starts over.

"I have a fiancé and I think he might be cheating on me."

My heart sinks. Not another one. I hold in my distasteful sounds and make an "uh-huh" noise. She launches into a diatribe.

"I never really thought he was the kind of guy to do something like this, you know? I mean, we haven't known each other that long, but it was like magic when we met—love at first sight. We've been so happy these past few months, and

I just"—*sniffle, sniffle, sob*—"I just can't believe he would betray me like this. I mean, I've put on a little weight lately, but these wedding plans are completely stressing me out! What does he expect—that it's all going to come together without any work?"

I hand her a box of tissues.

"Molly, the first thing to do is calm down," I say this gently, as though explaining to a toddler the reason she shouldn't pull the dog's tail. Her gasping sobs are starting to concern me. If she hyperventilates, will I have the strength to carry her to the car? Will the ambulance people die on my staircase when it gives out under the weight of three people?

"I deal with these types of cases all the time," I say. "I'm sure I can help you. First, we'll need to go over some specifics—some information about your fiancé: Where he works, where he hangs out after work—that type of thing. Also, I'll need photos of him."

Molly nods and takes another handful of tissues.

The rest of the meeting goes as expected. There is further crying and gnashing of teeth, exclamations over how much her fiancé loves her and how she really can't grasp the fact that he'd cheat on her, etc., etc.

I listen and nod, making sympathetic noises. I take notes while she talks and end up with a page full of information about one Jordan Shumly, her potentially-dabbling husband-to-be. We fill out a contract and she gives me half of the fee upfront using her credit card.

After she leaves, blowing her nose into the last half of my tissues, I start a new file, adding a copy of the credit card receipt, the contract, the informational sheet about Mr. Shumly, and two photos she's left with me.

Chapter Twenty-One

I spend the evening with my laptop, catching up on record keeping and updating the website. The statistics tell me it's time to run another sale. Last year I had a Valentine's Day special where I offered ladies half-price PI services for the week of the fourteenth. It ended up being quite popular, sadly. Sneaky men let their guard down around that time of the year, enamored with secret girlfriends, late-night trysts, and purchases of expensive jewelry. I'd made a bundle, though my gut felt tight each time I snapped pictures and documented comings and goings. My work isn't always sunshine and tulips.

The phone rings around ten, just as I'm getting ready to bring a new book to bed. I debate answering—it could be Creepy Caller again—and then snatch up the receiver just before the answering machine gets it.

"Hey," Ezra says. "Was wondering if you wanted to get together for lunch or something this week. I had that thing I wanted to talk to you about."

"Oh, right. The Thing," I say, walking to the kitchen where I keep my day planner. "Sure. Your turn to buy, right?"

He laughs, but agrees.

"I've got time tomorrow afternoon if you don't mind an early lunch. I have an appointment in the morning in Williston and another in the early afternoon with a new client back in St. Albans. I could meet you in town around eleven-thirty?"

"Yeah, sure. That sounds good."

We chat for a few more minutes about nothing and then hang up. I change into my flannel pajamas, wishing for the one-hundred-and-eightieth time that I had a woodstove in my bedroom, and curl up around a hot water bottle. I fall asleep with the book on my chest, three pages in.

***

Early the next morning, I follow the I-89 south to Williston. Jordan is an assistant branch manager at First Choice Bank. I plan to spy on him and see what I can learn.

Finding someone who doesn't want to be found involves skill, patience, and creativity. Finding someone who doesn't know they should be hiding is significantly easier. Jordan, I'm wagering, is as clueless as he is cute. Something like sixty percent of affairs start in the workplace, so that's where I start. I debate trying to get in to see him personally, but in the end decide it's easier to just go in with an inane banking question and scope out his workplace.

The atrium is stifling hot. The tellers wear sleeveless dresses and dressy tank tops, chatting away behind a high granite counter. I walk to the kiosk full of deposit and withdrawal slips and peruse pamphlets on mortgage rates and car loans, surreptitiously taking looks around. Glassed-in offices frame the main area. Jordan's office is positioned on the west side of the building. It looks out over the parking lot, my lucky day.

I walk to the counter and ask the mint-sucking woman about opening a checking account. While she talks, I glance at Jordan's office. He's seated at an expensive-looking desk, talking into the phone and pecking at his computer. I can see where Molly might worry. In comparison to her gently-rounded figure, Jordan looks like he works out a minimum of fifteen hours a week. His starched shirt fits perfectly over a flat abdomen and broad chest. His hair is brown and shiny, like Christopher Reeve in his prime.

I turn my attention back to the teller, nodding, smiling, and murmuring something about thinking it over, then stroll past Jordan's office, pretending to inspect an ugly painting near his door. "…can't right now. I want to also, but—" he sighs, lowering his voice. "…I know."

It would be weird to stand here any longer. The bored-looking security guard might suddenly come to attention. I wander out of the front door, brochure grasped in hand. The cold slaps me across the face like a rich but classless reality TV wife.

Back in the car, I wriggle down in my seat and pull out a small pair of powerful binoculars. I train them on the building, finding Jordan's window easily. The job of the assistant bank manager, I decide after nearly an hour, is freaking *boooooring*. There is only one bit of excitement when an athletic-looking woman with long brown hair strides into his office.

I picture for a minute that we're in a Hollywood movie and the woman will straddle him and stick her tongue down his throat. Instead, she talks for a few minutes, hands him a folder, and leaves the office, crossing to her own across the atrium. I can't make out the writing above the door, but the office is bigger and more luxurious than Jordan's. Athlete Woman must be the bank manager.

I watch Jordan inspect the file, give a small smile, and begin to type again on the computer keyboard. Fifteen minutes later, he stands, stretches, and makes a show (or is it my imagination?) of checking his watch. He pulls on a thick wool pea coat and leaves his office, nodding and smiling at the tellers who bat their eyes in response. Then he walks out a side door opposite the parking lot. I keep the binoculars on him, but when he goes around the building a tall hedge hides him from view. Where is he going? A mid-morning walk? A rendezvous?

I scoot out of the car, tuck the binoculars into my coat pocket, and start walking on the wide sidewalk until clearing the front of the bank. Then I stoop and wedge myself into the thick line of cedar hedge. Snow tumbles down in clumps around me and a little makes its way down my coat collar. I shiver, bat at it, and then stand to full height. I'm thankful that the spiders who make these branches home in the summer are all dead now. Branches poke me in uncomfortable places, but the shrubbery makes a good hiding spot.

Pulling the binoculars back out, I scan the area where Jordan was headed. He's standing near the rear corner of the building, a small shed and a little, fenced-in area nearby. He's watching the corner of the bank that he'd just come from.

Footsteps sound nearby. I hold my breath. The security guard from the bank? Or maybe a second one who only patrols the exterior of the building?

Branches poke and jab me. My mittens feel too hot, and I can feel my palms sliding around inside them, clammy with sweat.

The footsteps draw closer.

Then I hear a deep voice say, "Hey, what are you doing?"

Chapter Twenty-Two

My heart hammers in my chest so hard that I half-expect it to flop right out. I want to sprint from the spot but my legs are frozen in place.

"Hey, man, it's been a long time," another voice says. "Whatcha been up to, bro?"

I slowly exhale as two guys try to outdo each other with MTV-sounding phrases. Is MTV even around anymore? The popular TV station used to be the center of my universe. My breath has returned to normal by the time the two have finished discussing girls, "sic" rides, and their newest job perspectives. I wait until they've moved on completely before following the hedge around the side of the bank, keeping an eye on the building itself.

Small, dark globe cameras dot the exterior. I push my way back into the hedge, closer to the shed.

What's that? A flash of black against the white snow: Jordan's coat, ducking into the small structure. I wait. The hiding spot smells like a winter wonderland, branches and bark scratching my wrists and neck. Keeping the binoculars focused on the shed door, I nearly jump when Athlete Woman appears suddenly, full screen in the enlarged image. She's smirking as she enters the shed, dark hair streaming over her shoulders like a shampoo commercial.

Eight minutes later, Jordan emerges, looking as pristine as when he arrived except for the untucked button-down, which he shoves back into the waistband of perfectly-pressed khakis. He rubs a hand over his shirt front, then buttons up his coat which was hanging open. How can they not be concerned about the cameras? Can Athlete Woman turn them off? Do they not cover that area? Or is the risk part of the fun?

I press the 35mm camera's button over and over, getting shots of Jordan fixing his shirt, smoothing a hand over his perfect hair, and checking once over his shoulder before I lose him around the side of the building.

I wait another three minutes and Athlete Woman emerges, looking (if possible) more perfect than Jordan. She isn't tucking anything in, though the rather slinky, stretchy dress likely doesn't have even a pocket. She, too, is buttoning up her coat, the cold in the air making a frosty cloud in front of her face. I take more photos of her and realize as I zoom in on the last shot that there's not only a huge, honking diamond on her hand, but a wedding band, too.

***

A drug store in Burlington still offers one-hour photos and 35mm film development. I could use the kiosk and my digital camera, but I like to do these things old-school.

The woman at the counter smiles at me and tells me to be back in forty-five minutes, as things are slow. I wander around the store for a while, looking at gaudy nail polish, neon hair extensions, and foot cream.

Forty minutes later, I tuck the package of glossy images into my bag along with a scrap of paper with some general details on it—date, times, mileage, and an abbreviated version of what I'd seen. All of these notes will be typed up neatly in a full report for Molly, which I'll turn over to her along with the photos and a bill for the second half of my fee.

Maybe she'll have further use of my services. Marketing to someone who's just had their world torn apart feels pretty slimy, but I like to think of it as helping a heartbroken woman through a difficult time. The fact that I charge her for services rendered is just part of business in the real world.

***

Ezra is five minutes late and looks disheveled when he meets me at the restaurant. This is not our usual pizza or sub joint, but a real, honest-to-goodness, *nice place* with tablecloths and everything.

"What's the occasion?" I ask, waving a hand around the half-filled dining area. "Did you get a raise or something?"

"Huh?" Ezra's head pokes up from behind the menu. Oh, did I forget to mention? It also has real menus, not the type written on a big board that gives you a crick in your neck from looking at it while waiting in line to order.

"Oh, yeah. I mean, no. No raise. I just thought it would be nice to have a little quiet and privacy to talk."

"That sounds ominous."

Ezra grins and the tightness in my belly loosens.

"It's nothing bad. Just some things I've been thinking about and thought I'd seek your wise counsel on."

I snort while sipping my water and it nearly comes out of my nose.

160

"You must be desperate."

He grins again, his head ducking back behind his menu.

We place our orders a few minutes later. Ezra goes for a bacon burger made with local beef and I throw caution—and my newly-formed healthy eating habits—to the wind, ordering a plate of fish and chips.

"So, what's up?" I ask, extracting a piece of the soft bread from a basket lined with a thick, white napkin. The bread is fresh from the oven and my mouth waters before I've even finished buttering the slice.

Ezra takes his time responding; glancing over his shoulder, grabbing a slice of bread for himself, and adding a thick coat of butter before he speaks.

"I've been thinking about leaving the brotherhood."

I nearly choke on the bread which is lodged neatly against my windpipe. I scramble for some water. I drink nearly the entire glass before I can speak.

"What?" I finally croak out. "Are you serious?"

He nods, then shakes his head. "No. I'm not sure. But yes, I'm considering it. I don't know if it's the right thing to do… hence the counsel-seeking. But I've been having these feelings lately and I want to explore them, I guess."

"What kind of feelings? Ezra, this is"—(*crazy, nuts, off-your-rocker worrisome*)—"I don't know what to say."

"I know. Crazy, right? I just…" He breaks off, looking out the large bank of windows. "I don't want to make the wrong decision. This is going to affect the rest of my life and if I choose wrong, it'll screw things up." He pauses and takes another bite of bread, chews, and swallows. "This must be how regular guys feel before they propose to someone."

I sit motionlessly. If he'd told me he was pregnant, I couldn't have been more surprised. This is all he's wanted for a long time.

Finally, I rouse myself. "Are you sure it's not just nerves? You're getting close to the end of your time as a brother. Maybe you're just nervous about taking your vows for the priesthood."

"Maybe. But there's something else." He leans toward me. His hair is wavy and dark and there is a piece of blue lint hanging precariously from one strand. "I'm worried about, you know, marriage and kids and stuff."

"Huh?" No one ever accused me of eloquence.

Ezra sits for a few moments in silence, the slice of bread in his calloused hand halfway to his mouth. His dark eyes look toward the windows and for just a few seconds, light from the sun fills the space and illuminates him. He looks like he's glowing and I realize for the first time in a long time—maybe years—how much I depend on him. How much of a sure thing his presence is in my life. If he leaves the shrine, will he also leave the area? And since when does he want a wife and kids? Did he meet someone?

There's a sinking feeling in my belly. I take another sip of water, wishing my wine had arrived.

He's talking again and I shake myself mentally, trying to focus.

"I thought this was my calling—I was sure it was. But lately, I've just been thinking more and more about the rest of my life. Do I want to spend it alone? Serving in a congregation where I get to see inside other people's lives but never invite anyone into my own? It seems lonely."

"Well, there's always the cleaning woman," I say. Bad joke.

Ezra just smiles at me and shakes his head.

"Sorry," I say. "I'm just…at a loss for words, I guess. Or the right words, anyway."

We sit in silence for several seconds.

"How long have you been thinking about this?" I ask.

"A couple of months."

Months? This is worse than I'd expected.

"And you're just now seeking my wise counsel?"

"I wanted to be sure it was actually an issue. That it wasn't just panic or cold feet, like you said."

"And is there a certain girl who made you start to question your future vows?"

He sits in silence for a minute, chewing. The woman at the table nearest us throws her head back in laughter, interrupting the light jazz momentarily.

When he responds, "No," all the air in my lungs comes out in a whoosh. I cover it by coughing. What counsel can I give, wise or not? The fact that he's even asking my opinion says a lot about Ezra. His level of trust in me is much higher than my own.

"Maybe you should talk to one of your superiors. Not Father Benoir, but there must be someone else you could confide in."

Ezra nods, swallows.

"The thing is, part of me doesn't want to confide in a priest because, ultimately, isn't their job to get me into the ranks? Priests are a dying breed." Ezra rubs a hand over his face. There's a piece of white medical tape across the back and feathered scratches extending beyond the plastic. Suddenly I want to grab his hand across the table.

"Most of them are at or close to retirement age and new, young guys going in…well, it's not happening. At least, not much," he says.

I clear my throat and tuck my hands in my lap. "Maybe a

counselor, then? Or a pastor at a different church?"

I take a big swallow of the wine our server delivers as Ezra takes another bite of bread, chewing thoughtfully.

"That's not a bad idea. Someone at another church would have a better perspective, maybe. At least they'd be a little further removed from the situation. Yeah." Ezra nods, and then a slow smile spreads on his cheeks. "I know one in the area that I could ask. Yeah," he says again. "That's a good idea."

"You don't have to sound so surprised," I say.

He flicks his fingers against mine. "Thanks."

"Solving problems is what I do," I say, taking another swallow of wine.

Chapter Twenty-three

What is wrong with me? For the eightieth time, I wish that Sophie were a *real* sister, someone I could confide in. Why did I notice so many things about Ezra yesterday that I've never seen before? The way his hair waved, the scent of his aftershave—piney and spicy. And then there was that weird urge to take his hand in mine.

I punch the bag in front of me, shaking my head to get rid of the images and questions. *Focus on work, getting stronger, and losing these last ten pounds. Everything else? Forget it.*

The bag swings back and I plant another jab and then a cross-jab in rapid-fire. I do it again and again, alternating my punches with some kicks. The workouts haven't gotten a lot easier, but at least I can breathe through the pain now. Plus, I don't feel like crying after five minutes, so that's an improvement.

The cell phone nearby in my bag on the floor rings and I groan and try to look disgusted. Truthfully? A break from my workout is appreciated. The guy on the bag next to me grunts and plants another punch, the bag swinging in response.

I don't bother unwrapping my hands, but flip the cell phone over and see "number unavailable." It's the special pay-as-you-go phone that only receives calls for Sunflower Specials. I walk to a nearby corner, cover my free ear, and answer.

"Hello?" I say.

Nothing. Then some static and slow labored breathing.

"Hello?" One more try before I hang up. Probably some weirdo trying to get a thrill by freaking me out.

"This is Reba." There is more labored breathing and then a small sob. I press my free hand harder on my outside ear.

"What's the matter?"

"Leanne…" She breaks off and for a minute I think she's disconnected, but then I hear another small sob. "He…he hurt my baby."

I'm squeezing the phone so hard my fingers are nearly numb. Grabbing my bag, I walk quickly to the locker room.

"When?" I ask. My heart jackhammers in my chest. My gut is tight and sick.

"Last night. My husband won't call the police, says nothing happened, that Leanne was being a stupid teenage girl. But we're leaving, I told him. We're going—we should burn Prescott's house down first!" Reba's voice breaks. "My baby, my baby—" Her words turn into sobs.

I jam my arms into a coat and pull my keys from the pocket. "Where are you?" I ask.

She tells me and I nod, walking toward the door.

"I'll be there soon. Sit tight."

***

Thirty-five minutes later, I'm cresting the hill near Prescott's farm. I don't bother to slow down as I round a sharp curve and the tires spin out. I steer into the swerve and take my foot off the gas. The worst thing you can do on the ice is slam on

166

your brakes. That's unfortunate, since it's your first instinct.

The car corrects itself and I drive to a lower driveway, the one nearest the barn. A small, dark figure is hunched near a tree. As I approach, it walks toward me.

Reba, bundled in layers, opens the passenger door. I had time to stop by the office and grab my wig, and plaster a little makeup on my face, but now she knows what my car looks like. I don't care. There are bigger things to worry about.

She pauses for a moment, then looks back over her shoulder and nods. A second figure, smaller and even more hunched, walks toward us.

"Get in," I say to Reba, and she nods but waits for the second figure to draw closer. It's Leanne, bundled and stumbling in the snow.

I can't make out much of her face other than that it's pale and framed with red hair. Where Reba's hair curls naturally and springs around her face, frizzy and wild, Leanne's is glossy and long. She wears a knit hat, one with yarn braids that come halfway down her chest.

She doesn't look at me, just settles into the back seat and stares at her hands in her lap. Reba bustles into the car, rearranging herself and her layers until she can turn and look at her daughter.

"We're going to get you out of here, baby," Reba says.

Leanne doesn't respond.

I pull back onto the road and follow it to the state highway. There are no other cars out. The wind whips the snow around in small tornados. I turn up the heat dial but am only rewarded with lukewarm air.

"Are either of you hungry? We could go to McDonald's," I offer.

Reba shakes her head. "I don't want anyone we might know to see us."

I nod, following winding roads bordering frozen cow pastures and big farmhouses. Finally, we settle at a small café two towns away. It has grungy-looking, wood-paneled walls and I'm hesitant to drink the coffee I ordered. I take a small sip and look at Reba and Leanne sitting across from me.

Reba stares back, her eyes red-rimmed. Leanne traces circles on the table with an index finger. A question burns my esophagus and I want to blurt it out. But part of me doesn't want to know—can't deal with—the answer. Still, the words come.

"Is this because of what I did? When I went to his house…" The words come out fast and choppy and Reba is shaking her head before I even finish the question.

"He's wanted Leanne for a long time," Reba says. She mutters a curse word that aptly describes Prescott. "He was drunk this time, and…" Her sentence peters away.

Leanne's finger continues to move in a circular motion—drawing figure eights, I notice. Back and forth, around and back. She doesn't touch the mug of cocoa sitting in front of her.

"It's not because of you," Reba says, her eyes tearing. "But this time, I want you to fix him. We won't go to the cops—not because of Doug, but because she doesn't want to." Reba nods at her daughter. "They'd probably side with him, anyway," she says bitterly. "Even if they did a"—her voice breaks off and she takes a big breath—"a rape kit, he'll just say that she encouraged him, that she wanted it. So, this time you fix him good. Don't let him get away with this. And there's something else."

I nod. "Anything."

"You've got to take her for a little while. Just a few days. I need to get us a place to stay, find a job. There's some cash—I'll get it when Doug's at work—but I need a little time to get us set up somewhere new."

Leanne makes a small sound, like the beginning of a word. Her finger stops mid-eight and I find myself holding my breath. But then she lowers her head further, takes her finger from the table, and folds in on herself, thin arms encased in a purple sweater hugging her torso, head bent, red hair falling forward.

"Of course," my mouth says at the same time my brain is asking me where, when, how, and what I think I'm doing. "Of course, I'll help."

Chapter Twenty-four

The first rule of Sunflower Specials: never let a client know your identity. This is the point behind the pay-as-you-go cell phone, the disguises that I wear when I meet with clients, and the out-of-the-way places we meet. They are walking on the edge by hiring me; I'm walking straight down the middle of the path marked "illegal," so I need to keep my bases covered. I could lose my business. And I really, really don't want to go to jail.

I drop Reba off at the farm. She insists on walking from the end of the long driveway, but before she does, retrieves a bag from a nearby shed and stuffs it into the backseat with Leanne. Her voice murmurs something—prayers, condolences, or reassurances, I can't tell. Then she closes the door, waves to me, and turns her back to the car.

I wait until she's crested a small knoll to back out of the driveway. When I look over my shoulder to check for oncoming traffic, Leanne is huddled near the door, eyes downcast, holding the backpack like a life raft.

Where am I going to bring her? The thought has been ricocheting in my brain since I first agreed to help. My immediate thought is Ezra. In the state Leanne is in, though, and after what she's experienced, I can't see leaving her with a stranger, especially a man. Besides the fact that Father Benoir would have plenty to say about the temporary living situation.

I slow around a corner. The wind is billowing outside the window, pulling snow across the road in gauzy strips. My mother's house? But how will I explain Leanne's presence? Besides the fact that I can't tell her how I'm involved in all of this.

I follow the back roads toward home. Desperate times call for desperate measures, right? I'll just have to hope that Leanne and her mother don't slip up and tell someone how I'm involved in all of this.

"Are you warm enough?" I ask over my shoulder.

You could hear crickets in the silence that follows. It remains this way, me drumming my fingers on the steering wheel and occasionally clearing my throat, Leanne sitting mutely, until we arrive at my trailer.

"You live here alone?" Her voice is rusty, as though she hasn't used it in a while.

I nod, too surprised to find any words to respond.

She doesn't say anything else, but looks over the trailer cautiously from the back seat.

I get out and walk around to her side, pull the door open. She emerges seconds later, the backpack swinging around her shoulders. It bulges and I nearly offer to heft it for her, but don't. Babying her isn't going to take away what happened.

I trudge through the few inches of snow to the front steps and make a mental note to come back out and clear them and the path to the driveway. Turning the thermostat up as soon as we get inside, I leave a trail of melting snow in my wake. I pull my flannel shirt off and mop it up as Leanne watches.

"You can leave your boots there." I nod to a rubber tray near the door. I take my advice and deposit mine, too.

"Do you need some slippers?" I ask.

She shakes her head and slowly bends to unlace her thick winter boots.

When she's stripped off her winter stuff, she follows me into the kitchen and sits precariously on a bar stool.

"I'm making cocoa. Do you want some?" I ask.

She shakes her head but then nods.

"Okay."

I turn on the radio and some peppy jazz fills the air between us. In a way, it makes our silence seem that much odder, but I notice that by the time the teapot is screeching at me to *take me off the burner right now!* Leanne has unclenched herself just a little. I stir in the cocoa powder while looking out the window over the kitchen sink. My view of the backyard is trees, trees, and more trees. Winston and I had cut a lot away that first summer I was here, making space and light for the garden.

Crap.

I never checked in on him. Even though he's about thirty years my senior and a seasoned outdoorsman, I worry about him, that he will get hurt and I won't know till weeks later.

Leanne clears her throat. "What's your name?"

I practically jump, lost in my thoughts so much that I'd forgotten she was even in the room. And what to say? Tell her my real name and risk making matters worse? But, really, at this point, can they get any worse?

"Tatum," I say. "But everyone calls me Tayt."

I slide one of the mugs across the counter to her.

"Careful. It's hot."

Good grief. I sound like my mother. Of course, the girl knows that *hot* cocoa will be hot.

I feel a little itchy inside, as though the walls are closing in on me and I'm wearing a too-hot sweater that I can't get off. I'm stuck with her for how long? Part of me is ashamed of myself—she's just been victimized, for pity's sake. But the other half of me feels panic setting in. Other than Winston who arrives unexpectedly and at odd times, I rarely get visitors. And I like it that way.

My phone rings—the landline—and I welcome the break in awkward glances and rush to grab it. Half-expecting it to be the prank caller, I smile when I hear another voice instead.

"So, I'm on my way over," Ezra says. "I have someone I want you to meet."

My throat is suddenly very dry.

"Is this a canine someone?" I ask. He's talked about wanting a dog for months now, but would he risk Father Benoir's wrath?

Ezra chuckles. "No, non-canine and very human. A female human. Don't worry, you'll like her."

I look back toward the counter and see Leanne take a sip of cocoa. My cheeks are hot and my hand, I notice as I wipe at a smudge on the wall near the phone, is shaking.

"This isn't a good time," I want to say. But it's Ezra and he's bringing a woman to meet me. I remember his words at dinner the other night: "...thinking more and more about the rest of my life. Do I want to spend it alone?"

I'd asked him flat out if there was someone and he'd said no. He wouldn't lie. Not to me, his oldest friend.

Would he?

"Great," I say. I glance back at the counter. Leanne is studying the trees outside the window. "I have company, but it's fine. See you in a bit."

Chapter Twenty-five

As I hang up the phone, Leanne yells, "Moose!" and runs to the window. I follow her.

There is, indeed, a bull moose walking languidly in front of the row of pine trees bordering the garden beds. He stops mid-step as though he heard her through the glass and glances toward the trailer. His breath comes in big, white clouds and evaporates immediately. His coat is scraggly and pulled free in spots, like stuffing coming out of a kid's toy.

I've lived in Vermont a long time and have never seen a moose in person. *Where's my camera?*

Before I can move, though, he saunters across the yard and crashes through the trees and undergrowth like a freight train in slow motion.

"Do you see those a lot around here?" Leanne asks, still watching the swaying branches where the moose had disappeared into the forest.

"No. I've never seen one before."

The quick break in the silence is gone and the noiselessness resumes quickly. The radio has switched to news, and I turn it off. We've had our fill of bad news already. I flick on the television just to distract us from the oppressive *nothingness.* Leanne finds a spot on the couch and tucks her legs under her, sipping from the mug and staring glassy-eyed at the screen.

I watch her for a couple of minutes. Her face is even younger now that it's somewhat relaxed. She's pulled her long hair into a messy bun and her cheeks look rounder, more child-like. I imagine what it would be like if she were my little sister, just here for a visit, watching mindless TV and observing the wildlife. And then I think of Prescott's hands on her, holding her down....

I can't sit still any longer. I rinse my cup and tell Leanne that I'm going outside to fix something and will be back in a couple of minutes. If she hears me, I can't tell.

Bundled in a wool coat, mittens, a hat, and fleece neck warmer, I tromp around between the shed and garden. I find a stray tomato cage and try to yank it from the ground, but it's frozen solid. I pull the tops of some dead weeds from the ground. Mostly, I just let the weak rays of the sun, the sound of the wind breathing through the pine branches, and the smell of fresh air settle my nerves. The air is so cold in my lungs that they ache each time I inhale. I welcome the discomfort.

I think suddenly, unwantedly, about C.J. His self-satisfied face—perfectly handsome; so… well, *perfect*—flashes into my brain. I imagine his response to my telling him that Ezra has met someone, a woman. I imagine his fake condolences to me. "That's too bad," he'd say. "You and Ezra had a good run, but now it's over. Everyone knows a woman who is friends with a man loses her status pretty fast after he's engaged. I mean, what fiancée wants her husband-to-be hanging out with someone of the opposite sex?" Never mind that Ezra and I aren't, weren't ever…like that. Something sharp scrapes against my ankle and I gasp, mostly from surprise.

Flipping up my pant leg, I see a line of blood standing out

against the pale ghostly-ness of my skin. A thorn, long and jagged, protrudes from a waxy vine. I move to grab it away from my ankle and then realize how stupid that would be, given that my mittens are wool and easily penetrable. Instead, I start twisting my foot back and forth, trying to extract it from the tangle of thorn bush without doing further damage. Of course, this throws me off balance on the uneven ground and I start to fall, catching my balance just before I land in a heap near the dead cucumber vines.

It takes another few minutes, with much cursing and some mild sweating on my part, to finally get my foot out of the bramble patch. I'm bent over, hands on my knees, when I hear laughter nearby. Ezra, standing with his arms crossed over his chest, shakes his head back and forth.

"I know I said you get yourself into some strange predicaments, Tayt, but this is"—he pauses, eyeing the brambles and then my red, sweaty face—"stranger than usual. Even for you."

He sticks a big mitt out in my direction, offering a hand. I slap it away. Grunting, I throw my shoulders back and say—with as much dignity as someone in my place can— "I didn't hear you drive up."

"Parked near your cow."

"Huh?" I whip off a mitten and run it over my damp forehead and crane my neck in the direction Ezra's pointing.

"Daisy," I mutter.

"Does she visit often?" He makes the weird snorting sound that comes when he tries to hold in a laugh. I try to glare further, but my eyes are practically squinted shut at this point.

"Too often. She's from Brown's farm." I walk—no, limp—toward the house. "His stupid cows are always getting out of their pasture and for some reason always end up in my yard."

Ezra clears his throat. When I continue walking, he does it again, louder. I look back over my shoulder. His eyebrows are raised in a question.

I'd completely forgotten. His *lady-friend.* I need a minute. I stoop over my ankle, attempting to regain my (rather mutilated) composure. Seconds later, Ezra's legs appear near mine and he squats down, his hand full of tissue.

"Let me see."

I stand up and hike the pant leg up further. The air is bitter cold, but maybe it's helping the blood to clot. I don't look as Ezra winds the tissues like tiny tourniquets around the area. His fingers are rough with callouses but gentle. Several seconds later, he's done. I shiver, but it's because of the frosty wind blowing.

"You'll live, I think." He looks up at me, smiling.

"Thanks."

I stand there awkwardly until he rises to his feet.

"Come on," he says, pulling me toward the trailer. "Come and meet Shyla."

"Shyla?" I try—and fail—to keep the sarcasm out of my voice. *What is she, ten?* "That's a kid's name."

"Just come inside. You'll feel better when you're warm and off that foot. What were you doing out there, anyway?"

I sigh and grumble. Ezra shakes his head and walks toward the trailer, leaving me to my mood. Who is he to bring a stranger into my house when I'm not even there? My cheeks are hot and, though I didn't think it possible, my dark mood gets even blacker when I see the Holstein standing near my driveway, chewing her cud. I'm about to hobble toward her waving my arms when Ezra puts a hand on my shoulder and propels me to the door.

"You could have asked before you invited her inside," I say. My voice is bordering on petulant.

"Just come on." He holds the door for me.

I want to stamp my feet and yell and tell him that I don't want to meet Shyla or anyone else that he finds appealing. I want to remind him of his soon-to-be-taken church vows and that he's giving up a dream. And for what?

Mostly, I want to punish him for waiting so long to tell me about this. About her. I'm his best friend, but right now I feel like a stranger. Or, at best, like some distant aunt who gets the news last and only if the rest of the family feels like bothering to tell her at all.

I brush past him through the door and into the eat-in kitchen. Warm air blasts my face and my nose immediately starts running. I sniffle while shuffling around on the rug by the door, trying to extract my clogs and at the same time casting glances around the area to catch my first glimpse of her.

"You got any soda?" a voice asks. It's female and sounds pretty. I look up from my shoe extraction and catch my first glimpse of Shyla.

Not exactly what I expected.

Short, spiky hair, earrings running up the cartilage on both sides of her ears, a pouting mouth that is covered in a bluish lipstick. My mouth practically drops open when I see the diamond stud poking out from her cheek. Do people pierce their cheeks? She must be all of thirteen, though her attitude and facial expressions tell me she's much older. Or at least trying to be.

"S-O-D-A," she repeats slowly and more loudly, as though I'm an imbecile. "Do you have any?"

Ezra snorts from behind me.

CHAPTER TWENTY-FIVE

"Uh, no. No soda."

Shyla sighs and shakes her head as though I just informed her that there will be no more electricity for the next six months and we'll all be living in bunkers. She slumps toward the living room where the TV is still on, blaring more loudly than before. A judge is glaring at someone over her small glasses, making wisecracks while the plaintiff or defendant—I can't tell from here—chuckles and shifts uncomfortably from one foot to another.

"Where…?" I start to ask at the same time Ezra starts talking.

"She's a mentee. You know, through the Northwest Mentoring Program?"

I nod my head. It sounds vaguely familiar.

"They partnered you with a girl?" My clogs are finally off, and I hobble to the closest kitchen chair and flop into it. Why have my knees suddenly gone soft?

"Well, that's the thing. I can't *be* partnered with someone of the opposite sex. There was some confusion on their end—her name is sort of androgynous—"

"No it's not."

"Well, anyway. We've just met with the coordinator at NMP. They explained how this pairing won't work. I was actually hoping that—"

Realization hits me like a ton of proverbial bricks.

"Oh, no. No. You're not even thinking that I—"

"She's a really sweet girl. You'll like her."

"Yeah, she's made a great first impression. Though 'sweet' isn't the first adjective that springs to mind."

"Shh," Ezra says, and pulls out the chair next to me. I don't know why we bother lowering our voices, the TV drowns out any sound within a twenty-foot radius.

"She needs someone like you, Tayt. Someone strong and independent. You'd be a perfect role model for her. You can take her places or just hang out with her." He stops, motioning toward the living room with his hand. "They said that activities don't have to be expensive or extravagant. Just, you know, simple things like board games or going sledding."

I try to picture me and Shyla playing Monopoly in my living room. I shake my head, but Ezra keeps going. If he doesn't make it as a priest, maybe a traveling salesman isn't out of the question.

"She needs someone," he repeats. "She's sort of lost. In that weird place of teenage angst where it feels like the whole world is against you. You remember that feeling, don't you?"

"Yeah, but—"

"Just give it a try. What's the worst that could happen?"

"I lose the very small amount of free time I have, endure uncomfortable small talk, and spend hours trying to entertain someone who looks like she'd as soon eat me as play a board game with me."

"Don't worry. She's vegetarian."

I snort. "Great."

"Just think about it, okay? I'm getting a mentee, too. A kid I haven't met yet. We'll all hang out together. It will be fun." Ezra grins that same lopsided grin that he's had since childhood. It would make my mother swoon into action, granting whatever wish she could. This is how we'd ended up with so many stray animals at our house during the months Ezra had lived with us.

Now it makes me want to smack him.

Joint laughter comes from the other room. Ezra jerks around in surprise toward the sound.

"She doesn't laugh much?" I ask.

"No. I mean, yeah, of course she does. Shyla's a barrel of laughs. Who else is in there?"

Crap. I'd forgotten all about Leanne.

"Oh, uh, just a friend's daughter. I'm watching her for a day or two. Trouble at home."

Ezra raises his eyebrows. "See? I told you. You'll be a natural at this."

***

At eleven o'clock that night Leanne is once again in front of the TV. She did emerge, temporarily, to eat dinner at the kitchen table. Then she flipped through some magazines for a while because I told her that the TV had to be off for at least an hour. I'd never realized how noisy and annoying it was until I was forced to listen for hours on end. It was driving me nuts.

I'm not sure what I'm supposed to do. Should I enforce a bedtime? Offer to set up an appointment or two with a local counselor? How far is my role of temporary guardian supposed to go?

I leave Leanne with strict instructions not to open the door for anyone, not to answer the phone, and not to go out alone. I don't give her a bedtime but do ask if she needs anything while I'm out. She tells me she doesn't and pulls the thick blanket off the couch and over herself while I get my boots on.

A plan has been percolating in my mind, and I need to act on it.

I can't get Ezra's request off my mind, though, as I follow the winding road back to Prescott's house. Ridiculous? Yes. And not an option for me—not now.

With one hand on the wheel, I partially unzip my backpack and check the contents. Spray paint, stun gun, handcuffs, and rope.

Who says one's work-life can't be fulfilling?

Chapter Twenty-six

Sneaking into Prescott's house for the second time is much easier than the first. My brain remembers which boards on the stairs to avoid due to squeaks. And I was genius enough to remember a penlight.

A big clock downstairs announces that the time is nearing midnight. My breath is fast and light in my chest, my palms damp with sweat under nitrile gloves. I had to pick the lock this time, but the gloves are thin enough that I could leave them on to do the job. The air in the house feels stale after the freshness of the outdoors, but it offsets this with warmth, welcome on my cold extremities and cheeks. I stop every few paces, listening for sounds of movement. There are none.

In my pocket, the stun gun practically vibrates in anticipation. "Take me out and use me!" it says.

I swallow, a dry ball of fear lodged in my throat. This could go wrong on so many levels. I nearly glide down the hall, footsteps silent, ears alert to any movement.

No sound.

My hand reaches out to grasp the doorknob of Prescott's bedroom. Light from the moon pours through the window across from his bed. The curtains are only half drawn. How can anyone sleep with that much light? He is, though, his breathing deep, even, and heavy when I push the door open. Thankfully, it's the only sound; the door hinges are well-oiled. Extracting the stun gun from my coat pocket, I press the safety button to the "off" position and move toward the bed, cat-like.

At first, I can't make out his face. But as my eyes adjust, I see the smooth planes of forehead and nose, shadows crisscrossing everything underneath his nostrils. He looks peaceful, oblivious.

This is someone's child. The thought pops into my head suddenly. How do we all start the same, with downy heads and innocent hearts, but some of us turn so rancid and ugly inside?

This isn't the time for philosophizing, though. I close my own eyes for a second and picture Leanne in this man's grasp. His hard, strong hands holding her down. Her screams for mercy. Struggling to escape a fate that she didn't want. That no one does.

Heat bubbles in my gut like lava.

Ready.

I press a little button on the side of the stun gun. An arc of blue lightning cracks. Prescott jerks upright out of his sleep and I jam the little black box into his neck. His scream dies into a moan and then into nothingness within seconds. 100,000 volts of electric shock will do that to a person. His body slumps back onto the pillows. His eyes are closed but his mouth is partway open. Drool puddles onto the pillow.

My hands shake as I put the gun back into my pocket, remembering to put the safety back on first. I don't bother turning on a light in the room since the moonlight is so bright. Instead, I crouch and extract the materials I'd brought from my bag.

I'm breathing hard as I remove the rope first. Long lengths of clothesline—cotton, not nylon, which is too slippery. I strip off Prescott's shirt first—not an easy task. His arms are heavy and warm. Twice, we bump heads. By the time I'm done, I'm sweating. He wears only tighty whitey's down below and these are easier to remove. His belly has a line of thick curling hair running over it. He hasn't put on the weight that usually comes with middle age.

Prescott moans a little, quietly, and I start tying. Sliding the rope around each wrist first in the type of knot that won't come undone, then binding the rope to the bedposts. Left arm first, then left leg. I move around to the other side and repeat on the right.

I'm panting a little now, my forehead covered in a sheen of dampness. My shoulder is aching, pulsing with each heartbeat. I take a few seconds, hands on hips, and slow my breathing. Surveying the room more closely for the first time, I notice that it's not as untidy as the first floor. Not clean by any measure, or clutter-free, but neater. Flowered curtains hang from the windows and the dresser across from the bed has a collection of framed photos. I try to imagine Prescott here with his wife, the woman I saw in the sewing room last time I was here. Did she know he was a monster? Did she care?

Stooping to my bag, I extract the can of spray paint. I climb onto the bed, sitting to the left of Prescott's body, and shake vigorously, as recommended in the directions. A minute later, I stop. The silence is deafening after the metallic sound of the rolling ball mixing the paint in the can. I squint at the man's chest. Luckily he's not very hairy, other than the vertical strip down his middle. Carefully, with a hand steadier than I expected, I write the word *rapist.*

The paint is fire engine red, glossy, and wet. It's also perfectly fitting, though not perfectly straight, running across the muscles of Prescott's torso. Now for the *pièce de résistance*. I search through my backpack again, this time looking for a small white and green tube. Three, actually. Kooky Glue. I pop a pin in the end of the first plastic cylinder, then the next, and the third. Prescott moans a little and I half-wish he was awake to see what's coming.

I bend over him on the bed and squeeze all three of the small plastic containers between his legs. It dries nearly immediately.

Whatever he tries to do with his penis in the next week or so is going to be incredibly painful. I smile, then gather my things and leave the room.

***

By the time I get to my car, I'm shivering so hard that my key won't go into the ignition. The air is icy outside, but inside the car's interior, a modicum of heat remains. It's not just the cold that's making me tremble, though. Adrenaline, leftover with nowhere to go, leaks out of my fingertips. My teeth nearly nip my tongue between chatters.

He deserves it. He deserves it. He deserves it, one half of my brain repeats. The other half reminds me of Ezra's words in the café the night we went to the movies: *"Revenge doesn't feel as good as you think it will."*

Part of me wishes I'd never taken Reba's call. Another wishes that Prescott had been awake to see what I'd done. That I'd hurt him more. I wish…

Thunk!

CHAPTER TWENTY-SIX

Something hits the side of the car so loud and hard that I scream.

Beside me in the wide driveway is a bull. At least I think it's a bull—clouds have passed over the moon and I'm momentarily blind. I can make out the dark outline of a hulking shape. It looks more like a buffalo. I will my fingers to stop shaking long enough to get the stupid key to turn and finally—*voila!*—am rewarded with a growling muffler and lukewarm air blasting in my face. Turning the lights on, I see that it is, indeed, a bull, larger than any I've ever seen. What has Prescott been injecting these animals with, steroids?

I pull my seatbelt on and snap it into place, then put the car in first and get ready to floor it. The bull, apparently enraged due to high beams in his eyes, is pawing at the ground. I smirk in response and put my foot on the gas. The car shimmies, whines, and then stalls.

Are you *kidding* me?

Bully the Bull—maybe he won't seem so scary if he has a sweet nickname—stares at me through the window with something like hate in his eyes. I think about all the movies I've seen regarding safety and wild animals. Even though this one is technically domesticated, surely the same rules apply. Should I continue eye contact, thus proclaiming my dominance? Or look away and avoid confrontation? Make loud noises, like beeping the car's horn? Play dead? What's the protocol for dealing with angry farm animals? Something that starts as a whimper turns into a hysterical laugh. Ezra's comments about strange predicaments bounce around in my head along with the words, "death," "dismemberment," and "goring."

I try the key again and again until, finally, the Toyota starts.

It sounds a little weird, like a Polka song might be starting in the rear end, but I ignore that. Bully, though, doesn't like the noise and starts to paw the ground again.

I put the car in reverse. Going toward the bull seems like a bad idea. This time, when I put my foot on the gas, I do it gently. Perhaps I can coast out, like a gentle, harmless butterfly in the breeze. I glance in my rearview mirror, making sure the driveway is clear (it is, hurrah!), and then back away from the bull. He's lowering his head. *Paw. Paw. Paw.*

I keep on coasting backward, eyes on the mirror, repeating to myself over and over, "Butterfly in the breeze, butterfly in the breeze."

When the bull throws himself (literally, there is no other way to describe this than a throw) into my car the next time, he hits the right fender. Apparently, he's not a fan of butterflies. The car shimmies and shakes and for one awful second, I think it's going to collapse. I picture it like a tinker toy, falling apart into a thousand pieces and me, left in the driver's seat that is no longer attached to anything, smiling and waving at Bully.

But the car stays together. Mostly. I hear a metallic clunk and then the car's exhaust system becomes a thousand times louder than before. I don't let that stop me from accelerating at breakneck speed, though. The car slips and skids once on a curve in the driveway, but I turn into the skid, and it rights itself without sending me into a nearby snowdrift.

Finally, there is a little space where I can turn around. I whip the car into it and then pull out, heading toward the main road. I glance in the rearview mirror, eyes wide. The bull is running after the taillights, full force. Heart jammed in my throat, I remove my right hand from the steering wheel long enough to put the car into second and then third gear. The bull is still coming. Like a bad traffic accident, I can hardly tear my eyes away from the rearview mirror. But I do because not watching where I'm going is going to result in me seeing Bully up close and *very personal.* I hear a noise behind me, a sort of strangled roar (do bulls roar?), and press harder on the gas.

Finally, after making the tight turn out of the driveway and onto the main road, the beast gives up. I check my mirror again two more times, half expecting to see Bully standing on his hind legs and flipping me the bird. Or a bull's version of that. But there is only a blank, pale blue landscape.

If my fingers were shaking before, they are now jumping on the wheel. Still, a big, fat smile pulls at my lips, and I let out a whoop.

I did it! I did it! I did it!

Flicking on the radio, I sing at full volume to a Beatles song and do a car dance in my seat the rest of the way home.

Chapter Twenty-seven

The next morning, I walk up the road to Winston's house. I'd made a batch of muffins (Betty Crocker helped, but I did the stirring) and they're warm in the basket in my arms. The sun is bright, bouncing off the surface of the snow and glittering like a thousand shards of diamonds. Birds tweet and fly overhead, looking for stray seeds and whatever else they eat this time of the year.

A crow follows my progress from the top of a crooked fence post, and I pull one of the muffins free and toss it in his direction. He hits the snow so fast I never see his wings open. *Caw, caw, caw,* he yells into the air and then grabs half the muffin in his beak and retreats to a nearby tree.

I'd just talked to Reba, filling her in on her former boss' fate. She'd laughed so hard she'd started to cry but that had turned into sobbing, which took most of the joy out of the moment. Still, she told me I'd done well, and that meant a lot.

I'd let myself in last night without waking Leanne. She'd fallen asleep on the couch, bundled in blankets, a trail of orange cheese dust from a crumpled bag of chips nearby lining the pillow. Over breakfast, I'd asked if she wanted to walk up with me to the neighbor's, but she'd declined, instead taking a hot shower and settling back in for more daytime TV.

The tall fencing around Winston's homestead is coming into view, bent and crooked after years of abuse by the elements. There isn't barbed wire around the top, but it wouldn't look out of place. I sneak through a side of the fence where I'm just able to squeeze through—a spot that Winston had pointed out to me needed repair months ago.

A giant pig, spotted black and pink, heads in my direction, and behind it, a pack of wild dogs. Well, maybe not wild. They bark and yip while the pig out front, leading her troop, snorts, snuffles, and makes a high-pitched whining sound. Winston takes in all the strays he finds—or rather, that find him—even though I've told him time and time again that it would be better to call the local animal shelter. He doesn't have room for them in his maze-like house, but has built a small colony of ugly (but sturdy) dog houses outside. Besides the houses, the yard is strewn with automobiles in various states of rust and dotted with a few old appliances. The dogs bound up to me, barking, and I clutch the muffins to my chest more tightly.

"Miss Piggy," I say loudly enough to be heard over the cacophony of barks. "It's just me, Tayt." The pig waddles up closer, snuffling and snorting, and then, in some language that only animals understand, gives some sort of signal to the pack of dogs, calling them off.

I give Miss Piggy a scratch between the ears and she moans, leaning into my thigh so heavily that I nearly lose my balance. When she waddles away, I manage to pet two of the dogs, but the third one shows me teeth when I move my hand in his direction.

The front steps are covered in snow, which means Winston hasn't been out in the past two days, at least.

Guilt blooms in my belly as I walk up the stairs, feet

crunching loudly in the snow.

"Winston?" I call out, banging my free hand on the door. "Winston, it's me, Tayt. Hello?"

I wait a few minutes, stamping my feet to keep the blood moving.

No answer.

"Winston?" I put my hand on the knob and feel it jerk beneath my fingers. Involuntarily, I step back, nearly tumbling down the wooden stairs, but catch myself at the last minute on the railing. Winston stands at the door, bleary-eyed and disheveled. Well, more so than usual. His shirt is torn on the edge, hanging over pants that are covered in grime. His hair is wild around his head, like cotton balls that have been pulled apart and then starched.

"Get in, get in," he says, grabbing my coat front and hauling me through the door.

"What the—" I stumble on a rug that's twisted underfoot and the basket of muffins falls to the floor.

Winston doesn't seem to notice.

"Did you see 'em?" He's looking wildly over my shoulder at the closed door.

"See who?"

"Snipers. 'Bout four of them. Been in the woods the last three days."

I sigh and bend over, retrieving the clean muffins still ensconced in the basket and setting them on a nearby counter. I pick up the dirty ones, about to dump them in the trash, when Winston grabs one and starts eating it.

"That's been on the... never mind." I toss the rest and watch my neighbor for a minute. He devours the muffin like he hasn't eaten in days.

"Winston, when did you eat last?"

"Huh?" he says around a mouthful of blueberry. "No time for that."

He continues to watch the door as though expecting it to fly open in his face.

"Do you want some tea?" I ask and pull on his arm. It feels hard as rock beneath my hands, muscles frozen. When he gets like this, the adrenaline floods his system, making everything too tight. He told me once in a lucid moment that afterward, he's sore for days.

"Winston, come on. Come sit down. The snipers aren't going anywhere."

I start water in the teapot that is always kept on the stove and search the cupboards nearby for the tea canister.

"Should bring the animals in, I should."

"They're fine. Miss Piggy is keeping everyone safe, don't worry."

Winston finally moves to the table a few minutes later and sits facing the door, eyes red-rimmed and overly bright.

Several minutes later, I bring the tea to the table, along with a plate and a tub of butter I found in the fridge. Winston hasn't moved, except his jaws, which are working on a second muffin. I pick the remainder of it up from the table which is littered with binoculars, maps, sketches of mechanical things, and old newspapers, and place it on a clean saucer I found in the cupboard.

I want to ask how long this episode has lasted but don't. He won't know the answer, anyway.

Winston, in my unprofessional, un-psychologically-trained opinion, suffers from some sort of schizophrenia or maybe PTSD. In fact, I found pills once on his windowsill in the kitchen when visiting and had asked him about them. He'd said that they were from a friend's doctor, that they were given to him after he'd had an "episode," but that he'd only taken them for a little while because they made his brain feel gummy. "Like I'm half-asleep," he'd said. I never saw the little vial again.

Most days it's more like dementia. Then, occasionally, a bad time like this when he is sure that people are coming to kill him, or cats by the hundreds are living in the walls of his house, or there's strychnine in the water supply. This is why he's created a sort of live-in bunker, complete with fallout shelter and about two years' worth of food supplies. Unfortunately, when he's having one of these episodes, he forgets that and stops eating after the cupboards and fridge are bare.

Without a phone, he can't call me if he needs help. And our houses are far enough apart that other forms of communication only include walking or driving to each other's house—though smoke signals probably aren't out of the question.

"Do you need anything?" I ask, refilling his cup of tea.

His hand shakes a little as he brings it to his mouth. His lips pooch out, blowing on the steaming liquid before he sips. He shakes his head.

"Animals okay, or does anyone need feeding?"

"Yup. Need food. Too dangerous out there now, though, Tayt. Too dangerous. When I saw the first man in the woods, I drug out the rest of the bag of food for the dogs and threw down some grain for Miss Piggy. But we'll have to wait until they're gone 'fore we go out again."

For a second, I think he's talking about the animals, then realize it's the snipers. Winston is toying with the handle of his mug of tea, rubbing a big, calloused finger up and down the ceramic. Every time his thumb hits one of the chips, it makes a soft scratching sound. I watch the tree branches outside the window for a few minutes.

"We'll just stay in here, then, till it's safe," I say. From the corner of my eye, I see the old man nod.

The snow, in a puffy layer like marshmallow fluff, glitters in the sun. Warm beams come through the very tops of the windows, the rest blocked by old, mismatched, wooden shutters.

"Why don't you go get some rest?" I say, patting his arm. "I can hold down the fort for a while."

He shakes his head.

Though the house is cramped with things—boxes, army bags, and equipment that looks like it belongs in the shed—it is clean and tidy. At least Winston isn't one of those hoarders who has dead rats or cats beneath piles of stuff. He even has logbooks, which he showed me once. He uses them to track all his inventory.

The sound of his thumb on the mug begins to slow. I glance over and see his eyes shut, but then the lids fly open, and he resumes rubbing. This lasts a few seconds and then the process starts all over again. I sit and look alternately between him and the window, pretending that I don't see the fight to stay awake. Maybe this is how mothers feel while watching their babies try not to give in to sleep.

Winston finally loses the battle, chin dropping to his chest. I wait a few more minutes, just to make sure he's out, then remove the mug from his hands and the saucer from the table. I find a flat-looking pillow on a couch in the other room and put it where the muffin plate was, then gently ease his head onto it. He may have fought the falling part but now that he's sleeping, it's deep and heavy. How many hours has he been awake?

I stand and then watch him for a few minutes. His back will be aching when he finally wakes up, but he's slept in more awkward places, I bet.

Putting the dishes in the sink, I walk to the basement. It's dark and chilly and smells musty with a faint odor of mothballs. I switch the light on at the top of the stairs, a bare bulb lighting the lower floor.

Shelves upon shelves line every inch of the space. The floor is concrete, as are the walls; both unpainted. Shelves are made from wood, metal, steel, and other materials that look like plumber piping. This is one of Winston's supply areas. Food in cans, boxes, bags, and tins lines each of the shelves. On the end of each storage unit is a clipboard with a checklist of some kind. This is apparently how he keeps inventory, but I don't know his system and his handwriting is even worse than mine.

I gather up some staples: rice, beans, soup mixes, a few dinner-in-a-pouch meals, some dry cereal, a tin marked "dry milk," and a bag of chocolate wrapped in black and orange, from last Halloween. At least, I *hope* it's last Halloween. I haul these upstairs, taking three trips as the packages are awkward and my shoulder starts to ache.

Setting the food on the kitchen counter covers the small amount of free space that was previously available. I lock the door behind me but don't close it yet. I'm not sure if he keeps the animals' food inside or out.

Ten minutes later, my hands feel like ice cubes, but the dogs and the pig are happily munching away on their food and wagging their tails. The water trough is full and I make sure that even the shortest dog has access. I even dug into the trash and retrieved the muffins for Miss Piggy, who gives an exaggerated sigh of pleasure as I walk by. I can't resist another scratch between the ears. She snorts again. I'd bet money she's saying, "sucker" in porcine.

***

There's a message on my cell from Ezra when I get home. I'd left it charging earlier and now listen as he asks if I've thought any more about the mentoring project and Shyla. I delete the message and stomp to the bathroom, brushing my hair so vigorously I almost smack myself in the face.

The last thing in the world I feel like doing is acting as a surrogate sister/friend/mother to some troubled teen. I need more time to think of a good excuse, though. Ezra is stubborn and won't give up easily.

Leanne is napping when I re-emerge from the bathroom. I call her mother on the landline phone in the other room, hoping not to wake the girl.

Reba answers on the second ring.

"It's me," I say. "Do you have any plans in place yet?"

There is a pause and then her voice, louder than I was expecting, "I'll pay you soon, I promise."

"No, that's not what I meant," I say, cheeks getting hot. I may not be a noble do-gooder, but she can't think I'm that heartless, can she? "I meant about your relocation plans."

"Oh." I hear an exhale on the other end. "Yeah. I think I've found something. I can't talk now, but I'll get Leanne from you soon, okay?"

Does she mean today? Next week?

"When do you think that might be?" I ask.

"Tomorrow, maybe. I'll call you. Can I talk to her? How's she doing?"

"She's…" What word best describes her daughter's catatonic state that won't make her feel worse? "She's resting a lot. She's okay," I say, and then add, "but she'll be better when she's with you again. A mother's love is healing."

Good grief, I sound like a sappy greeting card.

"Let me get her for you."

I leave Leanne to talk in private, closing myself in my bedroom.

Chapter Twenty-eight

Two days have passed since Leanne and Reba left. Reba had looked better when I saw her last: Stronger and more capable. Only her red-rimmed eyes had betrayed her inner turmoil.

Leanne had looked like a regular teenager, sullen and quiet, mumbling a thank you to me when her mother demanded it. I'd wanted to tell Leanne so many things—that someday she'd feel more normal, that this wasn't the end of hope—but the words had gotten stuck in my throat. Instead, I'd just smiled and said, "You're very welcome."

Reba had hugged me once, quick and hard. I didn't end up asking for the second half of the payment. I couldn't. Later, though, I'd found an envelope in my coat pocket. It had fallen to the floor in a flurry of green bills. I'd stared at them, a mix of guilt and gratitude eddying in my chest.

***

I get to the office a bit before noon. It feels, still, that I'm on autopilot. The last few days and all the drama surrounding Emerson Prescott have numbed me to my regular, everyday work. I spend the first several minutes arranging, dusting, and re-arranging the supplies on my hulking, green, metal desk, trying to ground myself.

Phone messages next: there's one from Henry D'Angelo, the owner and cook over at Big Daddy's Deli Delights, my favorite eatery. Why would he be calling me? I jot down the number after listening to the message twice, caught so off-guard the first time that I missed most of what he was saying. The second message is from Molly of the cheating fiancé fiasco. She asks that I call her back right away. The third message is from C.J.

"Hey, I was hoping we could grab some dinner tonight." Pause. "Call me."

I take the pink message slips and line them up in front of me like they do at a pizza shop. First come, first served. Coffee percolates away in the old coffeemaker while I call Henry.

"Big D's," says a baritone, Southern voice.

"Henry, this is Tayt Waters, returning your call."

"Well, well. The great Tayt Waters," Henry's voice is honeyed but his tone is joking. "You made it on to any of those TV crime shows yet?"

I laugh. "Not yet."

"Good, 'cause I need some help with a"—he lowers his voice to whisper—"situation involving my niece. Stop by for lunch and we'll chat about it."

I'm about to say that I have too much catching up to do, but my stomach is already growling in anticipation. Henry is more than a cook. He's a magician. I glance guiltily at the salad I packed from home.

"On the house, of course," he throws in for good measure.

"Sold," I say. "Be there in a half-hour."

I leave a voicemail for Molly and debate with myself before ignoring C.J.'s message. Just for now. I'll call him back soon.

***

There are no other cars in the lot when I pull in, so I park directly in front. Snow is swirling around in gusty circles as I jog to the door.

"Well, *hellooooo,* Ms. T," Henry says as I walk through the door. Henry is a big black guy from New Orleans. I've known him for years and still can't figure out if he's gay or just one of those guys who comes across as extremely effeminate. Today his girth is tucked into a pink dress shirt and checkered wool pants. A big, white apron covers it all and he's sporting what looks like a plaid hunting hat on his large, square head.

"Hey, Henry." I pluck a bag of salt and vinegar chips from the shelf and set them on the high wood counter. "How's business going?"

"Oh, you know. Can't complain. No one would listen if I did." He chuckles at this. "I'll feed you first and then we'll talk business."

I survey the big board above his head.

"What can I get for you this fine day, Ms. Tayt?"

"Can I get a Moo Magic Madness with extra pickles?" Unfortunately, Henry's creativity extends to his menu. Every item on the list is a tongue twister and he gets a certain pleasure in making you repeat your order until you get it right. Sometimes, when he's feeling grumpy, he'll pretend not to hear you, making you repeat it again and again. I've seen grown men—big, strapping construction workers—nearly brought to tears of frustration as they try and fail to place their orders. "Vermont Vital Vittles Wrap," "Charlie's Cheddar Charbroil," and "Bubba's Big Blue Cheeseburgers," are just a sampling of Henry's wordsmith finesse.

Despite the rather unappealing names, these sandwiches will make you groan in pleasure. And despite Henry's sadistic streak, he's a good guy. Eccentric, but good.

"So, whatcha workin' on now, T?" Henry asks, smoothing mayo onto freshly made bread. The smell of the yeasty dough turns the rumbling in my stomach to a full-grown roar. I distract myself by walking to the cooler nearby and studying the selection of bottled drinks.

"Same as always. You know, security gigs for the next American Idol wanna-be's, deadbeat dads, and cheating fiancés. What is it with men, anyway?" I grumble this last part under my breath.

Henry grunts in response, his focus on the sandwich before him.

"Do you know how many times I've been contacted by a man to check up on his girlfriend or wife? Zero," I say without waiting for an answer.

"That's because we're too lazy and cheap to hire you," Henry says. "Besides, if a wife or girlfriend cheats, a man tends to take care of that business himself."

"How so?" I ask, taking an orange soda from the cooler and setting it on the counter near my chips. Not my healthiest lunch ever. My watering mouth asks, "Who cares?" while a second little voice promises to eat just carrots for dinner.

"We have our ways," he says. I wonder for the hundredth time what Henry's real story is.

I'm distracted by his hands, though, in the process of layering on fillings. I watch, mesmerized. No matter how many times I've seen Henry prepare a sandwich, it's still amazing to see. Like an experienced ballet dancer standing on pointe, or an elderly sax player who has been playing since he was five, this man is a true *artiste.* His large, dark fingers set a thin bed of crisp lettuce on the bread, then a layer of perfectly ripe tomatoes, a smear of wasabi, fresh provolone cheese, and then the *pièce de résistance*: breaded and deep-fried roast beef. Finally, a drizzle of honey and expertly-placed dill pickles, then the top of the buttery, crusty roll. He makes these himself, every morning, so they're fresh.

The sandwich is wrapped carefully in white butcher paper, ends pulled taut with florescent tape, and carried to the register. Set gently down near the rest of my lunch, Henry's hand remains for a moment, as though blessing the sandwich before it goes. I thank him and grab a table near the window, the sunlight from outside pouring over me. Henry doesn't do plates and utensils. Just use the wrapper and don't whine about it.

The wind whips the sharp snow outside into icy tornados, blasting a trio of flannel-shirted men just coming in. They have that hungry, obsessed look in their eyes that practically *screams* Henry's sandwiches.

"*Helloooooo,* gents," Henry singsongs, and then the joking and ribbing begins.

I tune the men out, concentrating instead on the mix of warmth and cold, salty and sweet, of my sandwich. After the men have left and I'm sipping the last of my soda, ready to fall into a deep, food-induced coma, Henry lowers himself into the chair facing me. How the small, round bistro seat can hold him is a mystery. He grins at me as though reading my mind, white teeth flashing.

"Don't worry. I'm a lot lighter than I look."

I smile back and take another sip.

"That was so good, Henry."

"Mm, I get that a lot." He winks and for some dumb reason, I blush.

"So, what does your niece need?" I ask, ready to move the conversation back to business.

"All work and no play, Ms. T, makes for a very boring girl," Henry says, waving a finger at me. "How's that man of yours, anyway?" He takes a long, loud sip from a jumbo plastic cup with a tall, ridged straw.

"What man?"

Henry smiles lecherously. "You know, your tall friend. Handsome guy."

"C.J.?" I ask. "The trooper?"

Have we ever come in here together? I can't remember.

"Nah, not him. That boy looks like he's got a stick stuck somewhere you don't want to find. I'm talking about your other friend—you know, with dark hair. Little rough around the edges. Looks a little dangerous."

Oh.

"Ezra? You have a good memory. We've only been here together once and that was months ago."

"I've got a good memory for good looks," says Henry.

"Well, then it's no wonder you called me," I say. I've never met a man who likes to gossip as much as Henry. The fact that it's about my love life (or lack thereof), seems only to intrigue him more. He sighs like a kid whose mother just informed him that playtime outdoors is over. I ignore it. I don't want to talk about Ezra.

I pull a pad of paper and pen from my bag and flip the notebook open.

"You said you might need help with security for your niece?"

Henry wags his eyebrows at me but, not getting the response

he's hoping for, says, "Yes. Reggie. Well, her full name's Regina. She's my only sister's daughter." Henry pauses for another sip of his giant drink. "She turns eighteen this weekend and my sister hired a limo to take Reggie and a few close friends to Montreal. You know, enjoy their first drinks legally."

"I forgot the drinking age in Canada is eighteen," I say. I'm already madly searching for excuses. I know that there are mountains of bills to be paid and it won't be long before the letters from the hospital start to border on nasty. But doing a security gig for a bunch of screaming teenagers—no, revise that, screaming and *drunk* teenagers—in the heart of Montreal sounds like my idea of a nightmare.

"What's your rate?" Henry asks, setting his cup down on the table. "This is part of my birthday present, providing you as an escort. More of a gift to her mom, really," he says conspiratorially.

"Why not just go yourself? You look like you could handle a few street punks."

Henry laughs out loud and then shakes his head. "Come on, T. Do you honestly think I don't have anything better to do on a Saturday night than chaperone a bunch of squealing teenagers? Besides, Reggie would hate it. You'll blend right in, darling." He pauses, glances toward the door when the string of bells tinkle, announcing a new arrival. I'm not sure if I should be flattered or offended that he thinks I'll blend in with said squealing teenagers.

"How much?" he asks me again.

I frown, chew my lip. If I set the price high enough it might dissuade him. I do some quick math in my head and blurt out twice my normal hourly rate.

"Done," he says, sticking out a big hand for me to shake.

"And if you keep them away from the strip clubs, I'll give you a hundred-dollar bonus."

I shake his hand and force a smile.

This is going to be just great.

Chapter Twenty-nine

Molly's number comes up on my cell as I'm parking. I'd tried her before I left the office but had to leave a message. I answer on the third ring, hoping she's not going to dissolve into tears once again. But this time her voice is steady and firm.

"Thanks for calling me back," she says. "I'm hoping you could help me out with another job," she says. Pause. "It's a little unorthodox."

I think of Sunflower Specials. *If you only knew...*

"I'll try. What is it?"

She clears her throat. "I want to set Jordan up. Give him a little taste of his own medicine."

"Okay," I draw the word out as though it's made of many syllables. "So, what do you need me to do?"

"His bachelor party is Friday night." No wonder she was such a basket case. "And I have an idea...."

***

I spend most of Friday cleaning my house and worrying about Winston, who I haven't talked to but know is fine, since I saw him pass by on his four-wheeler yesterday. Who knows for how long, though? Next, I worry about Leanne and Reba; about Ezra and his request that I mentor what's-her-face and the *big decision* he's facing; and, of course, about the creepy caller-turned-stalker. Should I have shown C.J. the note from the gym? The thought has crossed my mind more than once, but I hate the thought of involving him.

I turn the music up on the little teal radio. Instead of drowning out the worries, though, the song lyrics just tangle up in them. For the first time in a long time, maybe ever, I wish I had a dog. At least it would be someone to talk to. Plus, he or she would need things that I would have to concentrate on, like potty breaks and walks and feeding schedules. Maybe I should ask Winston if he'd like to gift me one of his strays.

I sit back on my haunches, blow a piece of hair out of my sweaty face, and survey the floor. It's gleaming in the late afternoon sun, shadows from bare tree branches swaying across it as though they're dancing.

Dancing.

Molly.

Reggie.

Ugh.

Molly's Revenge—her term, not mine—commences in a few short hours. And tomorrow night I'm hopping in a limo with four girls headed for a night out on the town in Montreal. Maybe I was a fool not to pursue a career in acting. I could be sitting in a dressing room in New York City right now, having makeup applied and practicing last-minute lines.

I imagine it for a minute: The smell of the pancake makeup and hot curling irons and hair straighteners, the giddy laughter, and nervous adjustments of costumes. The sense when you step on the stage that you're fully alive. Fully present.

Because if you aren't in that moment, your audience won't be able to come along with you.

Stretching, I get to my feet. Feeling more like Cinderella than a Broadway actress, I set my scrub brush down and walk to the guest-room-turned-dressing room. The light in this room is dim and I notice that the overhead fixture needs a new bulb. It smells good, though, like perfume and possibilities. Rows of clothing racks line three walls, each holding tidy rows of clothes. There are tough leather jackets and hiking boots, jean overalls and flannel shirts, sparkly sequin skirts, and gossamer-thin blouses with plunging necklines.

The collection had started before I went to college the first semester; most of it was purchased at thrift shops, then, later, at some higher-end consignment boutiques. I push the thoughts of credit card bills out of my head and run a hand over a red silk dress. "If I'm going to be an actress," I'd told Ezra when he'd asked why my closet was so crammed with clothes, "I have to have a full wardrobe." Then he'd asked about the necessity of that, seeing as most theater groups *provide their actors with wardrobes.* I'd shaken off the question. Like so many other things, men just didn't get it.

I finger the hem of a mini skirt I've yet to wear. Tonight, my role in Molly's plan is simply to act as the getaway driver—and muscle if things get out of hand. That won't require a cute outfit, though. Automatically, I turn to a different rack of clothes, this one made up of wool, denim, and dark colors. Appropriate? Yes. Fun? Not as much. I stretch my back again and can't help but grin, thinking about Molly's plan. She's clever. And bold. I can't wait to see her fiancé's face.

There are still two hours before I need to get ready, my watch says. I'm about to call Ezra when the phone rings. Shutting the light off in the dressing room, I grab the receiver in the living room.

"Hello?"

"Hey, it's me." C.J.'s voice is warm as honey.

I picture him at home, stretched out on the extra-long couch, taking swigs from a bottle of local beer. He only allows himself two per weekend night. Not because he's afraid of becoming an alcoholic, but because he doesn't want to get a beer belly.

"What's up?" I ask.

"Nothing. Didn't you get my message?"

Oops.

"Oh, I'm sorry. It's been really busy and it just—"

"Slipped your mind," C.J. finishes my sentence and my cheeks flush. "I was wondering if you wanted to come over. Get a video or something."

What's the *or something?* I wonder, but don't ask.

"I can't, but thanks for asking. I'm going out in a little bit."

"Who with?" His voice is less honeyed, more hurt.

My shoulders automatically go toward my ears and my back stiffens.

"It's work, C.J. But even if it wasn't, that's not your business anymore. Remember the whole *friend* thing?"

He's silent for a long minute. I picture another long pull on a brown bottle.

"Sorry," he finally mumbles. "I didn't mean it the way it sounded."

I sigh. Apologizing doesn't come easily to him, I guess I should feel grateful.

"It's okay. I should go, though. I have to get ready."

"What's the gig? Or am I not allowed to ask even that?"

I miss the days when phones had curly wires you could

tangle in your fingers while talking. Or maybe strangle in a tight fist.

"It's a security gig for a bachelor…" I clear my throat. What man would hire a female security person for a bachelor party? "A bachelorette party. Low-key, small group. Should be fun." I make my voice sound enthusiastic.

C.J. chuckles. "Sounds like it. Alright, I'll talk to you soon, then. And Tayt?" he says before hanging up. "Be careful."

Five minutes later, I'm still standing in the same spot, phone cradle in hand. I chew my lip and stare out the window at nothing.

***

Two and a half hours later, Molly collects me from the Park and Ride in St. Albans. The not-so-happy couple had recently upgraded to a three-bedroom apartment in the upper part of the city. Molly told me earlier that she'd already packed eighty percent of Jordan's stuff into boxes and called a moving company to deliver his half of the furniture to his parent's house tomorrow. He had no idea this was happening, as he was staying at a friend's for the weekend.

The scent of expensive perfume wafts over me as I step from the cold air into her warm SUV. Though I usually prefer to use my car, jalopy though it is, tonight I'm making an exception. If I'm playing getaway driver, I want it to be in something trustworthy, and Molly's two-month-old Suburban fits the bill. Especially with its fresh, new snow tires.

"Thanks again for helping with this," she says.

I glance in her direction as I pull my seatbelt on. Her fingers drum nervously on the wheel.

"No problem," I say. "Were you able to get in touch with the escort service?"

She nods, checks both ways, and pulls out onto the main road.

"All set," she says.

She'd done a little sleuthing, found out which service was providing the stripper for the party, and canceled it, playing the role of concerned sister.

"What did you tell them?" I ask.

"That I was the groom-to-be's sister and that our mom just died. Shockingly tragic right before a wedding, isn't it?" She gives me a half-grin and refocuses on the road ahead.

Her beautiful cap of blond curls is tucked into a wig that is long and dark auburn. She's wearing more makeup than before, quite a lot more, but it's expertly applied. When we hit a red light, she sighs and bites her lip, her fingers still tap-dancing on the wheel.

I struggle to think of something to get her mind off of her nervousness.

"You said you're in marketing, right?"

Molly nods.

"Is that what you went to school for?"

"My undergraduate degree was in theater."

"Really? Me too."

We spend a large portion of the next twenty miles discussing plays and musicals we've been in and seen live in which theaters. We talk about where we each studied and reminisce about our favorite roles.

The time goes quickly and soon Molly is navigating a back road in Milton, south of St. Albans. The road is bumpy and gets worse as it turns to dirt. We bounce in our seats for the next several minutes, then Molly takes another turn, slowing on a hairpin curve shortly after. I make a note of the twists and turns, as we may be leaving in a hurry.

"This is our friend—well, Jordan's friend, Mike's—place," she says, and seconds later steers into a long driveway. I can't see the house from the road. We travel a few more seconds in silence and then the house appears. It's magnificent: A mixture of logs and stone. The roof points and swoops in at least three different spots, windows take up most of the front, and the landscaping, even in winter, is impressive. Bushes and shrubs are perfectly formed, winding paths lead to more private areas behind the mansion.

"Wow." What does this guy do for work? Drug pusher? Arms dealer?

Cars are parked in tidy rows along the opening of the driveway. The house is dark, but the detached three-bay garage is lit up and heavy bass pounds out. Molly turns around in the driveway, then parks with the SUV's nose headed toward the road, several car-lengths from any of the other vehicles. Easy out.

"Smart," I say, smiling at her.

She doesn't smile back. Her lower lip trembles and her eyes fill with tears.

"Are you okay?" I ask.

She nods, shakes her head. "I'm not sure. I can't believe I'm really doing this. I can't believe that he did"—she waves her hand over her head—"that."

"Do you need some time alone?" I ask this to be generous, but hope she doesn't. I don't relish the thought of standing out in the icy wind.

She shakes her head. "No. I'm okay." Fumbling in her purse,

she extracts a nip; some type of vodka I don't recognize, and cracks open the cap.

"Want some?"

I shake my head. "Better not while I'm working."

"Right." She tips the bottle up and its contents glug down her throat. She pulls it away with a wince and makes a face. "Let's go. I'll finish this on the way."

***

The garage feels like a sauna after the cold winter air. A large group of men stands around one of those plastic folding tables which is lined with red cups, several varieties of beer, and other bottles of liquor and soda. A fogbank of smoke hovers over everything.

The place is clean and tidy, with sheetrock and paint on the walls; the floor looks like newly poured cement and there are area rugs here and there. I'm guessing the homeowner doesn't use it as an actual garage. Either that, or they are even more anal about cleaning than I am.

Two guys extract themselves from the group and walk toward us. I draw my shoulders back, spread my legs a little, trying to make myself take up more room and appear larger than I am. Molly seems to shrink beside me, drawing into herself.

"It's not too late to back out," I whisper.

Molly shakes her head violently enough that I worry her wig might fly off.

"No," she says, and as if by magic, comes to life. She tosses the long hair over her shoulder and giggles at the two men approaching.

"I'm Honey," she says, putting a well-manicured hand out to the first guy. "Where can I put my stuff?"

"Honey, good to meet you," the older of the two says, stooping to kiss her outstretched hand.

I hold in a groan.

"Jeff can show you where you can"—he pauses, smirks at her—"freshen up."

I follow Molly, who is following the younger guy, Jeff, to a small bathroom off the rear of the space. He leaves us there and as Molly stows her stuff and makes some last-minute arrangements of hair and clothes, I go back into the large room to survey the landscape.

A guy shoveling chips into his mouth tries to hit on me and ends up choking on some salsa. I pound him on the back a few times until he nods, waving me off with a weak "thanks." There are twelve men present, and Mr. Fiancé will make it a baker's dozen. Small bachelor party. Maybe that's how the rich do it.

I head back to the table of beverages and single out the older guy who met us at the door.

"Sorry, I never got your name," I say, extending my hand. If he tries to kiss it, I'll punch him. He doesn't, just shakes it somewhat dismissively and replies, "Mike."

"Okay, while she's getting ready, I need to go over some details with you. There's absolutely no physical contact other than what—" I stumble, "Honey initiates. There will be no grabbing, swatting, twisting, tweaking, or other handling of the dancer, is that clear?"

"Crystal," says Mike, but already he's distracted by lights bouncing up the driveway. "Our boy is here," he yells and the bass fades to a normal-sounding throb while the guys at the table turn their attention to the garage door.

"The cake is over there," a male voice says.

I turn and find Jeff at my elbow. "I'm the best man," he says almost sheepishly. "Shouldn't, uh, Honey get in before Jordan gets in the door?"

"Stall him," I say. "I'll give her a hand."

The cake—a big, Styrofoam-appearing affair—is blessedly light. It's also on wheels. The guy who choked on the salsa shows me how they lock into place. Seconds later, Molly emerges from the bathroom wearing a knee-length, silky robe. She looks pale in the dim light but no longer scared or shrinking. Instead, she practically dances over to the cake. I smell the alcohol on her breath before she's a foot from me.

"I switched to gin," she says and giggles. "This is going to be fun!" She tosses her arms over her head and grins at me. "My most original role!"

"Just hurry up," I say. "Lover Boy arrived, and his best man is holding him off."

Molly cranes her neck toward the front door. Her hands form fists and she curses under her breath. I help her into the cake—which, cleverly, has a little door built into the backside.

"It's kinda cramped," she says, squatting inside the interior. "But it smells pretty good. Like vanilla. Do you think they did that on purpose?" She giggles again.

"Sure," I say distractedly. "Do you need anything?"

She shakes her head.

"Ready when they are."

I retreat to the bathroom and gather Molly's things, stuffing them into the bag she was holding. Then I put it by the garage door and head to the side of the room, close enough to keep an eye on her and take care of my other job, securing the premises.

I leave my jacket unzipped, wide enough for the men in the room to get a look at the holster holding my Glock and can of pepper spray.

Chapter Thirty

As long as I live, I'll never forget the look on Jordan's face. Lecherous grin turning to puzzlement and then horror as Molly slowly removed her robe, then her skimpy lingerie, and lastly, her wig. Blond curls sprouted out around her head while some of the more intoxicated members of the party hooted and made rude gestures. Jordan's smile had slipped, and then a look I can't describe pasted itself on his face.

Luckily, I don't have to describe it as I caught it all on film from a tiny digital camera I held in my palm during the festivities. Molly asked me to, fearing she'd be too distracted by her dance to get the full effect of her gift to the husband-to-be. Or husband-not-to-be.

We run out of the garage, laughing, Molly requiring me to prop her up halfway to the SUV as the vodka and gin do their thing in her system. She's nearly in tears as I wrap her coat around her and a blanket from the back seat over her legs. I drive down the long driveway fast and we hit a bump near the end that causes us to bounce up in our seats like popcorn, which makes us laugh even harder.

"Did you see him?" Molly asks between peals. "Did you see his face? Where's the camera?"

I wipe at my eyes and clear my throat, trying to get a grip and stop laughing. Fumbling in my pocket, I extract the camera and pass it to her. It takes her a few tries to find the playback button, but when she does, laughter shakes her body so hard that the camera slides to the floor. I catch it before it hits the mat and then readjust the steering wheel as we're drifting to the right of the road.

"Wow, that was incredible," Molly says a few minutes later, the laughter having died down. "It's like one of those things, you know, that you think about?" Her words slur a little.

I know what she means, though. One of those things you wish you'd do, that you see yourself doing over and over in your daydreams, but don't have the guts to do in real life. Choosing the *responsible* thing instead.

"It was great. Good for you for thinking it up," I say.

"You helped. I couldn't have done it without you. Oh, no," she says, searching the top of her head with her hands. "I don't have the wig."

"I grabbed it. It's in the back with your other stuff from the bathroom."

"Thass good," Molly says, her words interrupted by a big yawn. "I got up too early today. Couldn't sleep."

It's quiet in the Suburban for several miles. When I check my right-side mirror before getting onto the interstate entrance ramp, she's drifted off to sleep, a smile still on her lips.

***

I help Molly into her apartment and leave her keys in a little silver dish by the front door. She'd had the locks changed today, she'd said, in case Jordan was stupid enough to try to come back tonight. I lock up and pull my scarf tighter around my neck. It's a ten-minute walk to the Park and Ride.

The air is bitter. Stars prick the night sky, glowing and shiny against the darkness. The snow under my boots crunches so loudly it's all I hear, besides my breath. I pull my shoulders and neck deeper into my coat like a turtle.

I like being out at night or in the early morning when no one else is. The houses are dark, the sidewalks empty, and only occasionally a car or truck passes by, swishing on the snow-covered road. One weekend gig down and one to go. I picture Molly, curled into her down comforter, and have a strange thought: What if we were friends? I don't have any girl friends, just Ezra and C.J. If desperate, I guess I'd seek advice from my mother. If Molly and I had met under different circumstances—if she hadn't hired me—would we have been friends? I spend the rest of the walk thinking about it, imagining us going to theater productions together and signing up for a local drama group. It's a nice thought, but when would I have time to do all of that?

When I finally reach the parking area, my legs feel like giant toothaches. I can't wait to get into the car. I follow a skimpy line of vehicles to the Toyota. A huge, hulking beast of an SUV is parked nearby, hiding it from view. As I walk closer, the hair stands up on my arms and neck.

Someone has been in my car.

The driver's side door is open a crack and the car is sitting lower than usual. Part of me wants to jog forward to investigate. The other part of me wants to hang back to assess the area. I move closer to the car nearest me and wait.

No movement.

No sounds other than my breathing.

Carefully, I ease myself around the trunk of the nearby car, then squat down again when I see headlights pan across the lot. A dark-colored SUV pulls in slowly and starts heading in my direction.

Suddenly, it's three months ago in my mind. I'm back on that road, where the man who shot me had sat waiting. My legs start to tremble, and I steady myself with a hand on the bumper. I duck lower as the SUV passes by. It crunches in the snow, the tires making a grinding sound as they obliterate a chunk of ice. Then it stops.

No one gets in or out.

Wiggling my way around to the other side of the car, I rise to my haunches to see what's going on. Finally, the passenger's door of the SUV opens, and a man steps out. Age? Indeterminate, but by the size of the coat and jeans, I'd guess late teens or early 20s. I pull the Glock free from its holster. The weight of it in my palm is reassuring.

"…later, man," the guy says and stamps his feet in the snow. Smoke billows out of the SUV, following him like a snowy whirlwind. He walks to a nearby truck and hops in; then I see the press of a red tip, a cigarette, as he cranks the engine. The truck growls to life and the SUV starts making its way back to the entrance.

I let out a breath and stand to full height, walking to my Toyota. I'm being paranoid. The car is fine. I probably just didn't close the door hard enough. I slide the gun back.

But then I see the tires and realize I was right to be cautious.

Every one of the four is slashed, and when I open the driver's side door, the interior is wrecked. Bits of plastic and chunks of Plexiglas (or whatever covers the gauges in a dashboard) are strewn about like a piñata that's spilled its guts. The box of emergency gear I keep in the trunk is completely pulled apart: Mylar warming blanket shredded, packets of hand and foot warmers torn, snacks ground into the carpet and upholstery. The road flares and emergency roadside kit are gone altogether.

I sink into the seat, a long, disgusted sigh filling the interior.

***

I wait ten long and cold minutes before the police come to survey the damages and take my statement. Thankfully, the last part is done in the cruiser. Warmth never felt so good to me. I'd spent the waiting time hopping up and down and clapping my hands together to stave off frostbite. The officer went through the paperwork carefully, yawning only once despite the late hour and less-than-exciting task at hand. He even waited with me for the tow truck to come and load my pathetic wreck. I thanked him and hopped into the cab of the tow truck. It smells like fake pine trees and exhaust fumes.

"*Whoooeee,* you got someone mad at you, huh?" the driver says, climbing behind the wheel. His belly is so large, I'm afraid he won't manage it. He does, though, and we take off with a lurch. The heater is blasting, and I warm my still-chilly fingers in front of the vent.

"I guess," I say.

"Ex-boyfriend?"

"No."

"Husband problems?"

I sigh, look out the window. "None of your business." I'm tired and cold. I just want to go home, not get a love lecture from a stranger.

"Alright, alright. I see it's a touchy subject," the man says with a dull chuckle.

We ride in silence for several more minutes. When we arrive at the garage, there's a taxi waiting.

"I called it in for ya when I headed out," says the tow truck driver.

Guilt blossoms in my gut like a flower.

"Thanks," I say, feeling like a jerk. "That was nice of you."

He waves it off.

"You've had a bad night. Thought you'd like to get home right off, not sit around here waiting for someone to pick you up."

Not that I have anyone to call. Ezra would come, but it would be more than a half-hour drive. My mother doesn't have a car. I guess I could call C.J—but I dismiss that thought right away.

"Thanks again," I call over my shoulder. "I'll call the office in the morning for the damages."

He waves a big hand over his head and starts working on the chains around the tires.

Chapter Thirty-one

The next morning dawns dull and gray. It's Saturday, a time to relax. Instead, I'm antsy and irritable.

I wake early to the sound of a chainsaw, which sounds like it's just outside my window. It's not; it's far down the road. The harsh buzz reverberates through the cold air and gets under my skin anyway. I burn my tongue on my coffee and my finger on the pan while frying an egg. Finally, in a huff, I layer on clothes and outdoor gear (hat, mittens, scarf, and a second pair of mittens), and my boots, and head out for a walk.

As usual, the last thing I feel like doing is the most beneficial. Within a mile, stress leaks out of my system. The air, while bracing, is also invigorating, and I drink in deep gulps of it. My eyes water. My nose is freezing. But the sounds of the wind moving in the bare branches of the trees and the occasional tweet of a brave winter bird help me slow down, reassess.

If I had my trusty notebook filled with a good list and bad list, it would read as follows:

The good list: Finished, successful jobs for Phil and Molly. Payments for this month's gigs and the one Sunflower Special, plus my cut of Repo Renew, will more than cover my office rent next month and pay down some of my bills. And that's without including the money from tonight's French escapade. *Ooh-la-la.*

I'd say my money situation is fair to average at present. Cindy is working out well at Repo Renew. I've heard barely a peep out of her for two weeks now. The situation with Sandra Garrison, though irritating, resulted in a free plane ticket anywhere in the continental U.S., to use at my leisure.

Bad list: Sandra has yet to come through with the final payment. Should I try small claims court? By the time I pay for legal fees, I'll likely be out more than the money she owes me. And then there is my car, which is completely messed up. I have no wheels for who knows how long. I only carry the kind of insurance that protects other drivers—collision, I think—so I'll be paying for the new tires and repair to the dash out of my pocket.

And I'm still no closer to knowing who Mystery Psycho is. The police officer had asked me all kinds of questions—was there anyone holding a grudge, anyone that I'd been in altercations with, an angry ex who might be out for revenge?—but it didn't help narrow down the suspects. And I could hardly tell him about my side gig as a vigilante-for-hire. Anyway, I'm too careful with those cases to worry about anyone finding out my identity. What nags at me is motive. Who has it out for me?

In addition to the car, I can't help but feel that my poor handling of Emerson Prescott the first time around only added fuel to the fire and ultimately resulted in what happened to Leanne. Reba assured me that wasn't the case but my gut says otherwise. The whole situation remains on the bad list, and I still feel guilty about the money Reba had hidden in my coat pocket.

Winston straddles both lists; the good one, just because he is Winston, and the bad one because of his episode earlier this week. Will they become more and more frequent until he can't stay in the house by himself? In a coincidence weird enough to give me goosebumps (if I didn't already have a thousand from the cold air), I see a tractor coming my way, a familiar plaid cap bobbing toward me.

"How're you, Tayt?" Winston asks like it's a statement, putting the engine of the hulking machine into neutral so we can hear each other. A low shout is still required.

"Fine. You?" I yell up to him.

He nods in response and scratches a bare hand under the cap, making it move up and down. "Alright. You fed the animals the other day."

I nod. This is "thank you" in Winston-ese. How much of that day does he remember?

"It's no problem. How are you feeling?"

"Fine, I guess. Tired. Did you come inside?"

"Yes. You don't remember?"

He shakes his head, looks off across a meadow. "Nope."

I nod again, shift from one foot to the other.

"Need to borrow the Ford again?" he asks, and I start.

"How did you—"

"Heard it on The Box last night. Know your license plate."

Winston, horrible at many things, likes being social and making sense most of the time; he has a brain for numbers and engineering that constantly amazes me.

"That would be great, thank you."

He nods.

"Lift?" he asks, and motions toward the tractor.

"No, thanks, I'll walk. See you in a bit."

He nods again, puts the tractor back into gear, the engine putting and growling, then continues on his way.

I hope he remembers when I arrive that he offered to loan me his old Ford. I sigh and try to re-ground myself in the moment. Pushing away thoughts of Winston forgetfully leaving a pot on the stove and burning down his house and my mystery stalker the same way I push away the low-hanging pine branches in front of me. They release a strong woodsy scent. I breathe in deep, carrying nature into my lungs. The peace of the woods is a balm to my brain. I'm not ready to go back quite yet.

How would my life be different if I'd decided to become a park ranger or a forester? There are plenty of these jobs in the Green Mountain State. Or I could have left Vermont altogether, headed into the hills of Virginia or the real mountains of Washington State.

There's a quick, jittery feeling in my gut. Regret. Why? Because I'd spent so many hours perfecting the craft of delivering perfect lines and annunciating my words for audiences—and lost out on something else. That's how choices are, though, right? You can't say yes to them all. Saying yes to one thing means saying no to something else. I forget where I heard that, but it's true.

I'm regretting the trip to Montreal tonight. That's something I should have said no to. I hate huge crowds, especially without the proper security. Plus, I'll be trapped in the car with giggling girls for close to two hours. My stomach gives a little shudder of dread. I push the thoughts away and focus again on the smell and sounds of the woods.

****

That night, I'm once again in the Park and Ride, waiting in Winston's small Ford, a car nearly as old as mine but in better shape. The heater blasts.

My legs—free from pants and long underwear for the first time in over two months—feel naked. Instead, I'm wearing black leggings, a swingy black tunic, and my big, black boots with London Jack over each toe. I'd longed to pull on my "witch boots," as Ezra calls them—pointed toes, tall heels, and lace-up fronts—but high heels wouldn't be good in a fight. Not unless you're Lucy Liu and cartwheeling across a movie set to kick some bad guy booty.

The limo pulls in ten minutes later and I flick the interior light on and check my bag one last time. While Vermont has no concealed weapon laws, it's illegal to carry a gun across international borders without a whole host of paperwork. Besides, I doubt very highly that I'll need my gun tonight. I do have pepper spray, which I'll have to declare at the border. I won't bother mentioning the nightstick that fits easily into my purse and extends to nearly five feet when whipped open.

Climbing into the limo I'm greeted by four girls: one coffee-colored with long legs and a beautiful smile. Sitting next to her is a blonde who is pale and chubby. The third is a dyed redhead and the last an exotic-looking brunette with equally long legs as the first girl.

"I'm Reggie," says the first girl, the one with the pretty smile. "This is Chloe," she says, pointing to the blonde. Then she gestures to the redhead. "That's Samantha. And that's Vivian. And to be honest, we're not super excited to have you along. Nothing personal," she says with a smile and slides a cigarette between her teeth.

I smile back, forcing my cheeks upward.

"No offense taken," I say. "I'm Tayt and, despite what you think, I'm not here to pee on your parade." Four sets of eyes stare, unblinking. "Think of it this way: My presence allows you this opportunity."

Chloe giggles and smiles at me. "That's a great way to look at it."

I grimace in her direction and then settle back against my seat, closing my eyes. "Just pretend I'm not here," I say.

That's what I plan to do.

Chapter Thirty-two

The limo drops me back off at the parking area at nearly four o'clock the next morning. The sun won't be up for another couple of hours, but the moonlight is so bright that the lot is fully illuminated. I shiver my way into the car and drive home, bleary-eyed, ears ringing from powerful subwoofers. My clothes smell like an ashtray.

I replay the night in my mind, trying to stay awake. It was without incident: a blur of hot, pressing bodies dancing and voices yelling to be heard above the deafening music. Except for the one time I had to pull Reggie from a group of cocky guys trying to get her to drink something from a flask one of them pulled from his pocket, that is. She'd sulked when I pulled her away and I'd shot visual daggers at the guys, who melted into the crowd.

It took me and the limo driver three trips to get all of them packed into the car. I sat up front on the way back, the sour smell of alcohol laced with vomit too much for me in the rear. Though my body pulled me toward sleep, I didn't give in. Instead, I chugged down a coffee while the driver filled the big car's tank. I didn't ask where he'd been during our late-night romp down St. Catherine Street, but guessed he'd been frequenting the other nightclubs.

Now there is the sound of gravel against tires. I jerk my eyes open along with the wheel under my hands. The car had drifted toward the side of the road. Giving myself a shake, I grip the steering wheel and crack the driver's window. The air is brutally cold, but does wake me up.

Finally, what feels like hours later, I'm home. I maneuver the driveway, but something is wrong. The tires crunch on the hard snow and I turn off the headlights. I'm sure I left a light on in the entryway like I always do, but the trailer is completely dark. The trees are moaning softly, the wind bending their trunks and heavy branches as I cut the engine. I sit in the near silence, watching and listening.

Nothing.

No sound out of place, no strange shadows that shouldn't be there. I grope under the passenger seat and find my Glock. I crack open the door of the car, then get out, crouching low. The dozy feeling is gone. Instead, I feel sharp and overly aware.

I crab-run toward the right corner of the trailer, checking the ground for prints. There are tracks in the snow lining the driveway, but I can't tell if they are my old ones or someone else's. The moon ducks behind some clouds and for a moment the area is pitch black. I strain with my ears, listening.

Still nothing.

I listen to my breath for several seconds. And then, something—a bump or thump—coming from the house. I can't tell if it was inside or out.

Inside, maybe.

My heart races and I take deep, steadying breaths. My fingers on the gun's grip are freezing and I tuck the Glock temporarily into my jacket pocket and blow on my hands to warm them.

Another thump. Definitely from inside. I scuttle around the side of the trailer, staying low. *Please let the exterior motion sensor be covered with enough snow that it won't—*

The floodlight turns on, nearly blinding me.

Crap.

I run around the back of the trailer, hiding in a crevice between the deck and greenhouse. My breath comes in puffy white clouds around my head. There is complete silence from inside.

Then a creak. The front door opens. I want to look up to see who is standing in my doorway, but I don't dare. If he has a gun, it could be the very last thing I see. Instead, I scrunch deeper into my hiding spot and try hard to ignore my burning quads.

It feels like twenty minutes have passed but it's probably closer to two. The door creaks shut again. Is the intruder still on the front step? Maybe he's aiming down the barrel of a rifle. Or has he gone back inside? The trees whisper, boughs bending and swaying in a light breeze. The scent of pine needles and wood smoke and the icy smell of snow says that all is right with the world even though it's not.

Footsteps clunk down the front steps. Slowly.

I hold my breath. Leg muscles straining, I rise a few inches in my squat and peek above the deck. Between the bottom rail and the floorboards, I see boots. They are black and heavy. Above that, a few inches of jeans show. Nothing else.

Moving the Glock closer to my torso, I clench and unclench my fingers around the grip. The cold makes my fingers clumsy and numb. I position my finger alongside the trigger, listening. Watching.

Three steps left.

CHAPTER THIRTY-TWO

Two.

One.

Now the feet and legs are on the snow-covered ground and my teeth are chattering. I clamp them together, but the rest of my body isn't cooperating. My arms and legs quiver—from the cold, adrenaline, or fear I don't know. I draw in a deep, slow breath and rise to my feet.

A figure stands in front of the stairs, turned away from me, surveying the driveway. He is thin and tall and wears a dark, bulky coat. I slide a foot forward, then another, the cover of snow muffling my awkward approach.

A branch breaks in the woods nearby. Immediately, the intruder swings a rifle in the direction of the woods. In my direction, too.

"Don't shoot," I say in a voice that's surprisingly calm.

I inch forward another foot.

His gloved hands jerk at the sound of my voice.

He fires.

I dive for cover behind the deck. The sound of the rifle's retort bounces off every hard surface in the area. It echoes in the woods and hills beyond. A dog starts barking in the distance as I scramble to my feet and run around the other side of the house. The path is icy where the snow has been trampled down by my own feet in the past couple of days. It makes for a treacherous escape, but it's the only path open. Going back to the car, the road, to safety, makes more sense. Instead, I'm heading around the side of the trailer, hoping I'll have some advantage by being on higher ground. Here the yard slopes upward until the hill meets the forest. Grabbing at the side of the trailer as I pass, I get my footing back and sink again to my haunches, listening. My legs curse me.

More wood sounds: trees moaning, branches tapping, the wind stirring snow and blowing it against trailer walls and tree trunks. Other than that, nothing.

Then, crunching. Boots in snow.

I stop breathing.

Then silence again.

I poke my head out around the edge of the trailer so that I'm facing the driveway. I half expect to see the rifle pointed at my nose, but there is no one. The security light is still blazing. I don't see the man anywhere.

Then there is a sound. A clang, the sound that metal makes when it strikes other metal. A few other strange sounds that I can't define. More crunching footsteps. In my direction? I can't tell. Hunkering down again, I crab-walk again to the other side of the trailer and peek around the corner.

There. The figure is near the back deck, huddled down low, their back to me.

I raise my gun, arm straight in front of me. I'm not trembling now. I rise to my feet, locking my legs.

My finger is near the trigger, but I hesitate. Can I really shoot someone in the back? Gun this guy down in cold blood?

My shoulder aches where the still-healing wound throbs.

I can. I should.

But I don't.

"Whatever you're doing, stop." My voice is loud and commanding, surprising me. "Put the gun down and your hands above your head. Slowly."

The man stops, freezing in place before getting to his feet. His back is still to me, rifle hanging limply from his left glove. He hasn't let it fall to the ground, though. The wind flattens his pants against his long legs.

"Gun down," I say, more forcefully. My arms are shaking a little. I move forward.

The moon breaks free from the clouds completely. The man turns, slowly, and puts the butt end of the rifle on the ground. With his free hand, he removes a ski mask. Blonde hair, long and untidy, tumbles out and over the dark coat collar.

It takes my brain a few seconds to catch up. To realize that this isn't a man at all, but someone else.

"Sandra?" I say, taking two slow steps forward. It won't do to slip on the ice and sprawl in front of her, possibly shooting myself on the way down. I tilt the gun downward. "What are you doing?"

She is looking at me like a wolf eyeing an injured fawn. I involuntarily take a step back, and raise the gun again. At the same time, I quickly inventory the shadows and shapes on the back of the trailer. The propane tank. That's what she was banging on. Had she broken through its wall? If I shoot now, will the house explode? Even if she hadn't, I can't risk shooting toward the tank.

Sandra stares at me, her eyes dark, but there is enough moonlight to see the look on her face.

Pain.

Anger.

Hatred.

"Put the rifle down and move toward the light," I say, voice loud. I motion with my gun toward the security-lit portion of the yard.

She makes a noise somewhere between a laugh and choked roar and motions with her free hand in a sort of *calm down* gesture. As if in slow motion, the rest of the rifle follows the stock toward the ground.

My breath is caught in my throat, my heart banging away wildly, eyes straining to see every movement she makes in the dim light.

Two things happen simultaneously, so quickly that time seems to stop.

The first is that the security light, controlled by a motion sensor, blinks off. Complete darkness covers everything.

The second? I hear movement and then hear a blast as Sandra fires wildly in my direction. "Wildly" is the right word. Bark flies off a tree at least thirty feet away. I duck instinctively, throwing myself back toward the relative protection of the trailer. I can't see anything while my eyes adjust to the new lighting. I can still hear, though my ears feel fuzzy following the retort of the rifle. Boots crunch on snow, slipping and skidding toward me, and I fire in that direction.

She screams and then I hear a crash of some sort. My eyes can barely make out her shape now, hunched and fallen over a wheelbarrow that was propped against the greenhouse.

Is she dead?

Keeping my arms out in front of me, gun steadier now, I maneuver the icy path toward the body.

"Sandra?" I yell as I approach. I want to ask what she's doing here. Why she's trying to blow up my house. And, suddenly, realization dawns. Has she been the one following me? But why?

The rifle is propped on the ground, pushed into the snow for leverage. Sandra's left leg is bleeding, a dark pool spreading onto the white snow.

"Tell me what you are doing—"

She curses at me, then turns to look at me over her shoulder, her face snarled in pain and fury. "You don't even know who I am, do you?" Her breath is coming fast and jerky.

Part of me wants to make a tourniquet for her leg, the other wants to put another hole in her. I go with my first instinct.

"Tell me while I put something on your leg. We've got to stop the bleeding. Now."

She glances at her leg, as though surprised to see that it's still connected to her body.

"Stay away from me," she says. "You've ruined my life. Now you're trying to kill me."

I keep my gun hand trained on her, searching my brain for tourniquet options. None come to mind except my clothes. I peel off my coat, switching the Glock from one hand to the other and then back again after I take off a flannel shirt underneath. Leaving the coat on the ground, I walk to where Sandra is sprawled and rip the rifle from her hands, tossing it aside.

Tucking the handgun into my waistband, I rip my flannel shirt in two.

"All I've ever done is help you," I say. I pull her leg out straight.

More blood leaks out and she growls and falls back onto her shoulders. Her face is white in the partial moonlight and her lips are nearly transparent.

That can't be good.

Her teeth are chattering but not enough to keep her silent.

"C.J. was mine. He was over you. Why did you have to come back here and stir things up?"

My hands freeze mid-air. Words are forming but I can't get them out.

C.J...

"He loved me! Me. Not you," she screams the words, spittle

flying from her pale lips.

I cinch the cloth over the wound, pulling it tight—so tight that Sandra screams. I pull it just a little tighter, my hands slipping over the soft cloth, and make a double knot. The blood is already soaking through.

"You want to kill me because of C.J.?"

"I just wanted to warn you to stay away from him. Because I can make him happy. I did make him happy, and he doesn't need you in his life messing everything up. Don't you get it? I was the rebound girl at first, but then he loved me. He did." Her head drops back onto the snow, her skin blending in.

"Keep pressure on that while I call 9-1-1." I stand up, a light sweat breaking out over my skin despite the icy cold air. I retrieve my jacket and slide my arms in. Sandra and C.J.? Why wouldn't he have told me? Why had she hired me?

Sandra turns her face away from me, but not before I see tears dripping down her cheeks.

"Let's get into the house. You'll freeze out here."

"Just leave me alone." She turns her face away from me, immobile.

I hesitate, then walk back to my car. I'll drag her into the trailer after I've called the ambulance. My fingers shake as I punch in the numbers, voice tremulous as I give dispatch my address and the nature of Sandra's wound. The dispatcher asks me to stay on the line. I tell her I can't and hang up. It might be faster for me to try to get Sandra to the hospital myself—

A shot rings out in the cold air.

Then another sound follows.

KABOOM!

I stare in disbelief as a fireball explodes upward from behind the trailer. I can't think. Can't move. Then my legs churn, racing around the house. The heat flattens me to the ground when I round the corner.

"Sandraaaaa!" I scream.

The entire back end of the trailer is gone, a huge, yawning mouth of fire and smoke in its place.

I crawl on hands and knees toward the flames. Sandra's form is slumped near the propane tank, her hand melded to the butt of the rifle like hot wax. Her face and hair are gone, her body limp. Flames curl around her like a tangle of blankets.

My screams have turned to moans by the time the ambulance arrives. I sit on the steps, rocking, rocking, rocking.

Chapter Thirty-three

C.J. sits across from me at Snuffy's, sipping a Pepsi and watching me. It's been days since the explosion, but every night my brain re-enacts the scene while I stare at the ceiling. We haven't talked, not really, since that night.

He shifts on the red seat, the vinyl squeaking under him. He looks…uncomfortable.

"There's something I should have told you before now," he says.

"Oh?" I ask, wiping my mouth and pushing my plate to the side.

He looks away, out the plate glass windows. The sunshine illuminates his face.

I wait for the familiar hum of attraction, for the old longing. But it's not there. How can that be?

I stare at his face—his beautiful, handsome, perfect face positioned over his tall, athletic body—and feel…nothing. Just a wisp of sadness.

"Me and Sandra. Well, we—"

"All set with that plate, hon?" Snuffy's mother bobbles her wrinkled face in my direction.

"Sure, thanks," I say and hand it to her.

"What about you, darling?" she asks C.J. with a wink. "Can I get you anything else?" Somehow the words sound lascivious, which is a little creepy coming from elderly lips.

"No," C.J. bites the word out and turns back toward me.

The old lady gives a little snort of displeasure under her breath and trails toward the kitchen with our plates wobbling in her hands. The restaurant is crowded, and I lean further across the table to catch everything C.J. is saying.

"Me and Sandra dated. For a while. She…" he pauses, looks out the window again, then toward the front door.

Anywhere but at me, I notice.

Realization dawns. I remember the way he'd reacted when I'd first asked him to see if Sandra had filed a missing person's report. The way he'd gripped the steering wheel of his cruiser. The way he wouldn't make eye contact. There had been an affair, that's why we'd split. And I'd never asked who it had been. Now, though, I thought I had my answer.

"She's the one that you slept with when we were together," I guess.

He nods.

"I never meant to hurt—"

"Oh, please, let's not go through all that again. I get it. I went to college. You were lonely. We've talked about it too much already."

"But not all of it. I mean, you never knew who it was."

"I didn't want to know!"

"But now, with what's happened, I just thought—"

I sigh, push back in the booth, and spread my hands out on the vinyl. How many times have we sat here? How many meals have we shared, first while dating and, within the past few months, trying to be friends?

Friends.

I snort.

"Okay. I get it. But why now, after all this time? She won. She got you and we broke up. What do I have to do with any of it? I should have been the one stalking her, not the other way around. Besides, it was years ago."

"We'd been in touch. Recently. I saw her shortly before that whole thing with her boyfriend—Mark, was it? She…" C.J.'s voice trails off for a minute and he finally looks me in the eyes. "She approached me at a bar. She was really off her rocker; I think she'd stopped taking her meds."

I nod. *Go on.*

"She wanted to get back together and rekindle things. We danced a little that night, had a few drinks. She wanted to come back to my place."

"And I'm sure you were happy to oblige." My voice is bitter. C.J. shakes his head.

"I thought about it. It would have been easy. But no, I told her I couldn't. Because…" He looks at me. "Because I'm in love with someone else."

I wait for the familiar hum in my belly, the warmth of C.J.-induced desire to spread over me, but I feel numb.

"So she starts stalking me," I say, "and decides to blow up my house because she can't have you?"

I hope he can hear how ridiculous this all sounds, but he simply nods.

"I think so. She was unbalanced, Tayt."

"Yeah, I noticed," I say and slide my arms into my coat.

"Where are you going?" he asks, moving with his hands to grab mine across the Formica tabletop. "You aren't just going to leave without saying anything. I just told you that I'm…"

His voice breaks off for a moment and when he starts speaking again it's lowered to a near whisper, "I'm in love with you."

I mash a wool hat with a green pom-pom onto my head and stand to zip my coat.

"No, you're not."

"Yes, I am," he says.

I lean across the table toward him. His eyes are shining and clear. I think for a moment about all the times I've looked there for solace. The many times I tried to convince myself he had what I was looking for.

"I think you're in love with what's comfortable, what feels familiar. But I don't want to live my life being someone's comfort blanket."

He sits, staring. He doesn't say a word as I turn and walk out of the diner, feeling lighter and freer than I have in months.

Chapter Thirty-four

"Where are y'all off to?" Mama asks, looking up from a home decorating magazine.

Ezra stands in the doorway while I put on a jacket. The temperature has risen considerably in the past few weeks. I'm down to just two layers of clothes most days. *Whoopee!*

"We're going"—I grimace—"bowling."

Ezra chuckles and Mama puts down her magazine and walks across the room to hug him. Then she slaps his arm playfully.

"You been thinking about what I said when we chatted?" She looks up into his face with a flirtatious smile. Mama, ever the beauty queen, just can't help herself around Ezra. Or any man, for that matter.

"Yes, ma'am," Ezra says, kissing her cheek.

I roll my eyes and shove my feet into combat boots.

Despite the less-than-glamorous destination, it feels good to be doing something out of my regular routine. Lately, "regular routine" has consisted of cleaning up debris, sifting through my possessions to see what can be salvaged, and spending far too many hours on the phone with the insurance company, contractors, and all the other people required to put my house back together again. If that's even a possibility.

I know I should feel grateful that Mama took me in. It's hard to move back into your parent's house, though, even after your own blows up. Here, I can never put things away properly or straighten the rugs the right way or clean the dishes to sparkling. To her credit, my mother never says anything. She just goes along behind me fixing everything the way that it "should" be.

We say our goodbyes and climb into Ezra's truck, which smells like pine needles (the real kind, not the fake pine-tree-air-freshener-type), and pull onto Route 7.

"What chat did you and my mother have?" I ask, pushing a piece of gum into my mouth. I hold the pack out to him, but he shakes his head.

"Oh, nothing."

"Mmm," I grumble, sounding sulkier than I'd like. I watch the houses pass by, one yard blurring into another. There is more green than white in most yards as the grass reclaims more and more of its domain. Why would Ezra confide in my mother instead of me?

"Does it have to do with your *big decision?*" I ask.

He nods.

"But I thought you'd already taken my advice. Why—"

"Tayt? Just enjoy the evening, okay?" Ezra's voice is relaxed, gentle.

I almost stop with my line of questioning.

Almost.

"Just tell me one thing and then I promise I'll shut up."

He sighs, but one corner of his mouth is already pulling into a smile.

"You make it so appealing," he says. "Alright. What's the question?"

"Did you ever find another pastor to talk to like I suggested?"

He nods.

"And did you get good advice? Do you know what you're going to do now?"

"That's three. Now shut up." He grins at me and turns up the volume on the radio.

I lean back in my seat and smile.

I'll get it out of him.

Some day.

***

The bowling alley is packed and, apparently, Friday nights are 80s-themed. Music washes over me in all its synthesized glory when we enter the cavernous room, the four of us grouping together to rent shoes and pay for three games.

Shyla is decked out in punk attire and looks like she just walked off the page of *Teen* magazine in 1981. She's wearing a jean skirt with florescent pink tights and a leather bomber jacket with a pink, mesh shirt underneath. She flirts with the guy behind the counter (who looks like a forty-year-old pedophile) and ignores Jason, Ezra's mentee.

Jason is heavyset and wears a tracksuit that looks two sizes too big, even on his bulbous frame. Ezra claps him on the shoulder as we head to our lane. I spend the game tossing my ball down the alley and listening to the wind whistle past before it falls into the gutter time and time again. Ezra nearly always ends up getting a strike and Shyla has the next highest score, though how she manages so many accurate attempts while checking out the boys in the lane next to us is anyone's guess. Jason is in third place even though he concentrates on the ball as though he can physically control it with his mind once it's released from his hand. Ezra compliments them both on nearly every attempt. I make mental notes to be a better mentor while inhaling a plate of nachos, waiting for my turn.

We finish the evening with ice cream sundaes at a local diner. Shyla tries to look like she's not part of our group and makes about fifteen trips to the bathroom. Ezra talks with Jason about a potential camping trip when the weather warms up. I ask Shyla if she would want to do a girls-only version and she gives me an eye roll in response. Ezra catches my eye and winks.

We drop Jason off first, then Shyla, before Ezra noses the truck toward my mother's house outside of Swanton. The night is warm and I crack the window, letting the fresh scent of starlight and melting snow permeate the truck's cab.

I close my eyes, listening to Janis Joplin sing-yelling in her famous voice about Bobby McGee. When the song finishes, I open them. We're on a deserted road that I don't recognize.

Ezra pulls to a stop. Does he see a deer? I look toward the tree line but see nothing.

"What are we doing here?"

"Come with me. I want to show you something."

Chapter Thirty-five

"Here? Now?"

In the middle of the night?

"Okay." I follow him from the truck, our doors slamming simultaneously. The sound feels sacrilegious in the still night air.

We tromp across part of a cow pasture, slipping and sliding in the slushy snow. I take deep breaths. My lungs ache from the pureness of the air.

"Do you know where you're going?" I ask after fifteen minutes. My combat boots are waterproof, but the thin socks inside aren't doing much to keep my toes warm.

"Almost there," Ezra calls over his shoulder.

We've moved into a wooded area, the sound of pine branches sighing above us. An occasional arborous creak and a single owl hooting are the only sounds. I follow Ezra's tracks. It's easier to maneuver in the snow, which is becoming thicker. We pause by a group of pine trees, Ezra putting out a steadying hand on one of the thick trunks. He looks over his shoulder at me and grins, slow and mischievous.

I smile back, feeling a strange warmth in my belly. I look down, eyes suddenly damp.

What would I do without Ezra? What if he's bringing me here to tell me that he's moving? Maybe he's changed his mind about leaving the Catholic church. He could have decided to try his luck at the Vatican for all I know, acting as a junior priest or some other type of underling. He's always wanted to go to Europe...

"Look. Right down there," Ezra says, motioning with a hand for me to grab. I slide my mitten into his glove, and we make a treacherous descent down a steep ravine to what looks like a black hole in the ground. Slipping and skidding in the mushy snow, I can't help but laugh at the spectacle we must make.

When we reach the bottom of the ravine, I start to pull my hand away, but Ezra either doesn't notice or wants to hang on. Shrugging, I follow him closer to the edge of the crater. Water is running. It reminds me of the fountain I have at home. Used to have at home. I suddenly wonder if it survived the blast.

Ezra says something and I give myself a mental shake.

"What?" I ask

Ezra crouches and points low.

"See the lights?" he asks.

I follow his outstretched finger but see nothing. Squinting, I zero in on the area he's pointing out to me.

At first, I only see the blackness of the bank. The crater is actually a little pond of some sort, and the water sounds are coming from the direction where Ezra is pointing. A waterfall, mostly frozen, trickles down an outcrop of huge, jagged boulders. In the spring the water must gush down in a river.

I train my eyes on the waterfall. Behind the ice I see lights, tiny, flickering, and yellow.

"What is it?" I ask in a whisper.

"Let's go check it out."

Ezra leads me, my hand still in his, around the bend in the pond and to the edge of the waterfall. When I was little there had been a series of caves behind our house that my brother, Max, and I had loved exploring. We'd spend hours out there, pretending to be pirates hiding secret treasure, or treasure-seekers looking for lost pirate booty. Sometimes we'd turn off our flashlights in the darkest depths and see who could make it out first.

When I was older, the caves were an escape from the world. When my parents were fighting or Sophie was winning yet another award for being her natural, perfect self or I got into a tangle with someone at school, I'd retreat there.

"Want to go in?" Ezra says. He finally releases my hand and it suddenly feels cold.

"Do you need to ask?" I say, already scrambling for a toehold in the large rocks.

"I can give you a boost," he says. I make it about three-quarters of the way up before agreeing. Ezra shoves upward on my bum and I practically launch into the cave behind the frozen falls.

"There's a whole room in here," I yell over my shoulder.

Ezra, faster than I was in my climb, is right there when I turn around.

"Pretty cool," he says, getting up from his knees and standing in a crouch in the space. His frame is too big to allow him to stand fully. I search the area for the yellow flickers of light that we'd seen.

Candles.

Fifty. Maybe more. I lean close and peer down. They are battery-lit, each giving off a soft, magical glow. Shadows dance on the cave walls and the ice glimmers. The only sounds are our breath and the trickle of water, dripping over the icy falls.

"You did this," I finally manage, turning in a wide circle, arms outspread. "You put all of these here?"

Ezra nods. He's smiling that goofy, slow grin that I love so much. I turn to look deeper into the cave and blink hard several times. Just when I think I know my best friend better than anyone in the world, he does something completely surprising.

"Do you want to sit?" Ezra motions further back.

I grab the tallest candle near me and head in that direction. My foot hits softness before my eyes take in two thick blankets, folded. I look at him again, smile and shake my head, then take a seat on one. Ezra sits on the other and for a few minutes we say nothing, just listen to the sounds of the water, the breeze that blows through the front of the cave, our own breathing.

Finally, Ezra breaks the silence.

"You know earlier when your mother mentioned that we'd had a little chat?" He goes on without waiting for a reply, "It was about you. About…" his voice fades for a minute. His profile in the candlelight is both rugged and boyish, serious and playful. I can see the pulse in his neck just above the collar of his fleece pullover.

"About us," he says.

I've stopped breathing.

"The reason that I've been thinking about leaving the brotherhood, about not becoming a priest, is because of you, Tayt. I think…" he pauses again and turns to look at me. His eyes are liquid in the light, shadows from the candles emphasizing his high cheekbones. "I think I'm in love with you. No," he says, shaking his head and letting out a big breath.

"I know it."

He grabs one of my hands resting limply on my thighs and pulls the mitten off, then removes his glove. Rubbing a finger gently over the back of my hand, he looks from it to my face.

"I'm in love with you, Tatum. I think I have been since we first met in junior high but was too stupid or scared to do anything about it until now. Until I thought of losing you. Again." He sighs and licks his lips. "I was trying not to feel what I did. But when you were shot I couldn't stand the thought that I might lose..."

This is wrong. Everything is spinning. My entire world was dumped upside down. Feelings I know I shouldn't have for my best friend tangling with C.J.'s voice and my burned house and Sunflower Specials. How can I keep that part of myself from Ezra? How would he feel about me if he found out? He's all about love and grace and forgiveness. I bite my lip, heart pounding like a bass drum in my chest. If he knew...

Taking a deep, shaky breath, I say, "There are things you don't know about me that you wouldn't like. Things that I've done. That I—"

"There is nothing that you've done or could do to make me stop loving you," Ezra interrupts.

I look at his face again and there is pain there. Real and raw and I hate myself so much in this instance that I want to scream. But how can I let him throw away his future—his dream—for me? How could I live with myself if I were the reason for him giving up something that he is meant for? Wouldn't he come to resent me someday, to hate me for it? And what is he even asking? I can't marry him. I can't be a pastor's wife.

I want to tell him this, all of it, but a sob lodges in my throat.

"Tayt," Ezra says it so softly that the sound of the splashing water nearly drowns it out. "I'm not giving you up. And I'm not giving up my dream of being a clergy member, either. I can do both."

The edges of his lips pull up. The candles continue to flicker, making a golden glow over his face. "I talked with Pastor Joe like you recommended. I met with him more than once. And I've prayed about it for weeks. Months. I've sought counsel with a mentor at the shrine, too. This is what I'm supposed to do. I know it without a shadow of a doubt."

I exhale, the sound loud and shaky in the small space.

"I mean, if you feel the same," he adds a sentence that feels like a question.

I stare into the candle flickering near us. The shadows play along the backs of our hands, mine small and white, Ezra's permanently tanned and marked with faint scars. Long-lasting reminders of his past.

A past that wasn't so perfect, a voice reminds me. I think of all that we've been through, independently of each other and together. And like a road, I see the future rolled out before me. Do I want to walk it alone to keep myself safe and protected from potential hurt, or walk it with Ezra? Do it imperfectly, get messy, and not know exactly what's coming next?

"I—"

Ezra interrupts, "Please, don't say anything now. Just think about it. Promise me that, okay? I know it's a lot to take in right now."

I nod.

"Okay," I say. "Okay."

Epilogue

I spend the rest of the spring overseeing the removal of the rest of my trailer. When they are done, there is just blank dirt where my house once stood. A clean slate, I try to tell myself, but the words "emptiness" and "loneliness" come to mind more frequently. The contractor will begin work in early May.

I wish they could re-build my personal life with hammers, saws, and hard work.

Ezra has been true to his word and not pushed me for anything. I thought things would be awkward, maybe even feel broken. But our lives don't feel that much different. We still hang out, see an occasional movie, grab a coffee, go hiking, or swim in Candlelight Pond. (I'd named it that, though in reality it probably has a stupid name like Cow Patty Pond.) Everything in my life has turned upside down and I'd asked Ezra to just be patient. And in typical Ezra fashion, he'd just smiled, nodded, and squeezed my hand.

Between managing the house demolition and plans for the re-build, I've also dived back into my securities work with a vengeance. I'm not sure what the future holds for Ezra and me, but whatever it is I don't want the heavy weight of debt hanging over me anymore. I haven't told him about the Sunflower Specials yet, but I won't give them up. Not now, maybe not ever. Maybe I will tell him about them someday.

Maybe.

***

This afternoon I have an unexpected break from work. I'm sitting on a boulder near the site where my new house will be built. The sun is warm on my shoulders, pressing heat through my t-shirt. Birds chatter above me and somewhere far away I hear the drone of a chainsaw. The air smells like earth and green things and worms. Holding a spiral notebook in my lap, I uncap my pen and start a list. Writing centers me and helps me to make sense of things. I go back to the lists I'd made mentally a few days before.

The Good List: Helping people with the Sunflower Specials. I think of Phil and Reba and Molly, who had all ended up as sort of a hybrid client. Molly and I have stayed in touch, and I think the beginnings of a friendship might be brewing. It feels strange to have a girl for a friend. She's so much fun that sometimes I forget she doesn't know me the way that Ezra does, that we don't have a history together.

Prescott was formally charged after further allegations from several families in the community. Sometimes it takes a single voice being raised, saying, "This isn't right," for others to join in. While the fact that there are children in recovery because of what the creep did definitely belongs on my bad list, I'm glad that Prescott is behind bars where he belongs. I toy with the idea of shipping him a big box of Kooky Glue.

The planning of my new house—okay, cabin—has been fun despite the trauma of losing so much in the trailer. Choosing plans for a new place and getting to decide all the details, while exhausting, is also liberating. And the increased security work means that I've qualified for a higher mortgage amount. I can get something bigger and with better resale value than the trailer had. Not that I'm planning to sell anytime soon. But who knows what the future holds?

I chew the end of my pen for a minute, watching the path of a robin hopping from branch to branch in a nearby tree. Returning to my list, I continue writing.

The Bad List: Failing Reba. The rape of Leanne will always haunt me. Sandra dying and the fiery explosion that decimated my home. Probably losing my friendship with C.J.

A short list, but bitter and dark just the same.

What's next for me? I don't know. And for the first time in a long time, instead of feeling anxious about that, I feel liberated, excited by all the possibilities. I've decided to sell the Repo Renew franchise to Cindy. She is excited about taking over permanently. There will be a meeting with our lawyers in a few weeks to make everything legal and signed on all the specified lines.

Workwise, I'll continue to focus on growing T.R. Waters Securities. I love the work, love to know that I'm doing good in the world. And the Sunflower Specials? I'll continue those too—for now, at least. I may not be a perfect vigilante, I may bumble as much as help sometimes, but I want to be there for people who have nowhere else to turn.

Because if I'm not there to help the next person, who will be?

***

AUTHOR'S NOTE: I hope you enjoyed Hear No Evil. Want to stay up to date on my next release? Sign up for the Readers' Club and you'll get a monthly behind-the-scenes look at my work as well as thriller and suspense book recommendations… and sometimes pictures of my cat. Thanks for reading!

Other Titles

Also by J.P. Choquette

Monsters in the Green Mountains Series
Silence in the Woods
Shadow in the Woods
Under the Mountain
The Pact

Stand-Alone Thriller Novels
Let the Dead Rest
Dark Circle
Epidemic

Tayt Waters Mystery Series
See No Evil, Book One
Hear No Evil, Book Two

About the Author

Thriller author, J.P. Choquette, writes suspense novels with themes of nature, art, and folklore. When she's not working, you'll find her sipping a hot beverage, reading, or in the woods with her family.

Join her Readers' Club and get peeks into her writing life, upcoming releases, and other treats for book lovers.

You can connect with me on:

🌐 https://www.jpchoquette.me

🔗 https://www.instagram.com/jpchoquette_author

Subscribe to my newsletter:

✉ https://www.jpchoquette.me